Rob's a...

on the bride.

With everything that was in him, with all the love he felt, he willed her to change her mind.

Jenny stood before the preacher, unable to concentrate on his words. She saw only Rob waiting on the hill above, trying to draw her to him by the sheer strength of his love.

All at once she knew she'd been wrong. The marriage ceremony wouldn't end anything. The pain wouldn't be over. It would just be beginning.

She would see Rob's face for the rest of her life. It would haunt her every time Jack made love to her, and it would be reflected in the eyes of the children that should have been Rob's. Even as she lay dying, Rob's face would be the last sight in her mind's eye.

"If anyone knows why these two people should not be joined in holy wedlock, let him speak now or forever hold his peace. . . ."

Dear Reader,

Happy Valentine's Day! Love is in the air... and between every page of a Silhouette Romance novel. Treat yourself to six new stories guaranteed to remind you what Valentine's Day is all about....

In Liz Ireland's *The Birds and the Bees,* Kyle Weston could truly be a FABULOUS FATHER. That's why young Maggie Moore would do *anything* to reunite him with his past secret love—her mother, Mary.

You'll find romance and adventure in Joleen Daniels's latest book, *Jilted!* Kidnapped at the altar, Jenny Landon is forced to choose between the man she truly loves— and the man she *must* marry.

The legacy of SMYTHESHIRE, MASSACHUSETTS continues in Elizabeth August's *The Seeker.*

Don't miss the battle of wills when a fast-talking lawyer tries to woo a sweet-tongued rancher back to civilization in Stella Bagwell's *Corporate Cowgirl.* Jodi O'Donnell takes us back to the small-town setting of her first novel in *The Farmer Takes a Wife.* And you'll be SPELLBOUND by Pat Montana's handsome— and magical—hero in this talented author's first novel, *One Unbelievable Man.*

Happy reading!

Anne Canadeo
Senior Editor

Please address questions and book requests to:
Reader Service
U.S.: P.O. Box 1325, Buffalo, NY 14269
Canadian: P.O. Box 1050, Niagara Falls, Ont. L2E 7G7

JILTED!
Joleen Daniels

Silhouette
ROMANCE™
Published by Silhouette Books
America's Publisher of Contemporary Romance

To Lorri Gentry for her help during the Great Printer
Crisis of '92;

To Russell and Bob Malone for being the best brothers
a gal ever had;

And to Beth and Perry Register—may your life together
be blessed with health, peace, prosperity and love.

 SILHOUETTE BOOKS

ISBN 0-373-08990-2

JILTED!

JOLEEN DANIELS

lives in Miami, Florida, where she tries to juggle a full-time job, a part-time writing career, an unmanageable husband and two demanding children. Her hobbies include housework and complaining to her friends.

If you can make one heap of all your winnings
    And risk it on one turn of pitch-and-toss,
And lose, and start again at your beginnings
    And never breathe a word about your loss;
If you can force your heart and nerve and sinew
    To serve your turn long after they are gone,
And so hold on when there is nothing in you
    Except the Will which says to them: "Hold on!"

If you can talk with crowds and keep your virtue,
    Or walk with Kings—nor lose the common touch,
If neither foes nor loving friends can hurt you,
    If all men count with you, but none too much;
If you can fill the unforgiving minute
    With sixty seconds' worth of distance run,
Yours is the Earth and everything that's in it,
    And—which is more—you'll be a Man, my son!

—Rudyard Kipling

Prologue

Landon Ranch near Layton City, Texas

In the next few minutes, the woman he loved was going to become another man's wife. And there wasn't a damned thing he could do to prevent it.

Rob Emory reined to a halt atop the hill overlooking the Landon ranch and surveyed the scene that was unfolding below him.

Wedding guests, dressed in their Sunday best, were gathered in groups near the refreshment tables, talking and drinking champagne. The row upon row of white folding chairs that had been set up on the lawn were unoccupied now. But soon the guests would file to their places, and the wedding would begin.

The groom and the minister would be standing under the gaily colored canopy at the end of the aisle. And then Jenny would appear.

Rob's hands tightened on the reins and the mare danced beneath him, sensing the terrible tension that coursed through his body. The wild, dark part of his soul longed to ease that tension, longed to swoop down the hill like a warrior of old and carry Jenny away. To ride over anyone or anything that dare stand against him.

All that prevented him from making that thought a reality was the knowledge that Jenny would never forgive him for it. He could take her body by force, but it would be an empty victory. He wanted all that Jenny thought, all that she felt, all that she *was*. There was no way to take those things by force. They had to be freely given.

So Rob did the only thing he could. He counted the passing seconds and he waited, hoping against hope that his very presence would cause her to change her mind.

And, as he waited, he thought back over the events of the past week, wondering if there was something he'd left undone, something he'd left unsaid that could have made a difference.

It had all really begun the night Jenny had come home from college. The night his brother, Jude, had married Margret Brolin....

Chapter One

Double Diamond Ranch near Layton City, Texas
A week earlier...

"You may kiss the bride."

Rob watched with a mixture of joy and envy as his half brother Jude took his new wife, Margret, into his arms to seal their marriage vows. Maggie's lovely face was radiant with a happiness that was mirrored on Jude's scarred, rough-hewn countenance.

To some, the marked contrast in their outward appearance could have been cause for comment or even ridicule. But Rob saw only the beauty of the love they had for each other. He himself had a face that more than one woman had called handsome, but at that moment he would have gladly traded any good looks he might possess for even a portion of the contentment that was shining so brightly in his brother's eyes.

When his new sister-in-law turned to hug him, Rob made the most of the opportunity. Letting his lips rest on Maggie's, he bent her backward over his arm and held the pose until she began to giggle uncontrollably.

Laughing himself, he released her and turned to Jude. His eyes filled with admiration and love, he gave his older brother a rib-cracking hug. "Well, *hermano,* at least now she knows who the *best man* is!"

Every one of the relatives, ranch hands and friends in the crowded living room groaned aloud. All except one.

Rob's head snapped around at the sound of a soft, familiar laugh. His gaze met Jenny Landon's and the moment seemed suspended in time. The noisy congratulations of the wedding guests receded as the sound of his own heartbeat seemed to grow louder. All the faces of those around him, even the room itself, took on a surreal, dreamlike quality as he focused on the reality of Jenny's features.

He moved toward her, maneuvering around those in his path with only a token awareness of their existence. He was aware only of Jenny. The laughter had faded from her finely drawn features. A faint blush climbed her cheeks as she watched him moving toward her, but her gaze never wavered from his.

After what seemed like an eternity, he reached her side. He stared down into her wide, gray eyes and lifted a hand to touch her dark red hair.

He couldn't have prevented the smile that stretched across his face even if he'd wanted to. His heart soared as he saw her mouth curve in response.

"Oh, Jenny..." Like iron drawn to a magnet, he bent to claim those soft, sweet lips with his own.

And then the dream turned into a nightmare.

"Jenny Landon, it *is* you! Congratulations on your engagement!"

Jenny blinked, unwillingly yanked back to reality by the effusive middle-aged woman who had seized her hand. For one unguarded moment she had let herself forget. She had let herself pretend that Rob was still within her reach, that there was still a chance for them. But now that moment was over—for both of them.

Her heart twisting within her, she watched all the warmth fade from Rob's dark Spanish eyes as he focused on the engagement ring she wore. The warmth was replaced by a blank stare that shut her out as effectively as if he had erected an unbreachable wall between them. She wanted to reach out to him, to do or say anything that would dissolve that barrier. Instead she made herself take a step backward, a step away from him. Then she turned toward Sybil Perry and forced a smile.

The older woman, the wife of lawyer Sam Perry, was still oohing and aahing over the size of her diamond. As usual, the local busybody's appearance couldn't have been more ill-timed. Jenny had planned to take Rob aside, to try to break the news of her engagement more gently. She'd forgotten about the damned ring. But maybe it was just as well that it had happened this way. The angrier Rob was, the more his pride was hurt, the less likely he'd be to pursue her. He had to understand once and for all that things were over between them. If only she herself could accept that one unacceptable fact!

Sybil was turning Jenny's limp hand this way and that, giving little gasps of admiration and envy as the facets of the pear-shaped stone caught and reflected the light. "Come with me, Jennifer. We simply *must* show this to Emmeline Davis."

Jenny hesitated, resisting the tug on her arm, waiting for Rob to say something, anything. Instead he turned away from her and blended back into the crowd. Tears threatening, Jenny stared after him. It had to be this way. She had no choice about that. But a small part of her wished that Rob had cared enough to put up more of a fight.

His thoughts in turmoil, Rob stumbled through the crowd of wedding guests. He had no clear idea where he was going or what he was going to do when he got there. But when a hand on his arm interfered with his forward progress, he turned on the intruder with a curse. He found himself face-to-face with his new sister-in-law and felt like the world's biggest fool.

"Maggie, I'm sorry. I didn't know it was you."

The expression on Margret's beautiful features changed from one of surprise to one of concern. Typically she wasted no time worrying about her own feelings. Her thoughts were all for him.

"Rob, it's not like you to snap at anyone that way. A minute ago, your smile could have lit up the room. Now you look like you lost your best friend. Who was that girl you were talking to?"

A ranch hand, who was setting up folding chairs around the perimeter of the large, cathedral-ceilinged living room, narrowly avoided stepping on the trailing train of Margret's dress.

Drawing her toward the center of the room, Rob tried to force a lighthearted tone past the anger, frustration and hurt. "I haven't lost my best friend, Maggie. You're right here."

Margret arched one expressive brow. "Then let me act like a friend. Stop trying to cover up. Tell me what's wrong."

One of the maids approached, carrying a tray full of champagne glasses, and Rob saw his opportunity. "Excuse me, but some lovely lady has been drilling me on etiquette for weeks now. I think I'm supposed to be toasting the bride and groom."

He winked at Maggie's annoyed expression. Grabbing a brimming champagne glass from the tray, he yelled for his brother. "Get on over here, Jude. I'm going to pay you a compliment, and I don't want you to miss it—it may be a long time until you hear another one."

There was a wave of laughter, and Jude Emory came up to stand behind his bride. "This had better be good, little brother."

Rob lifted the glass. "To Maggie and Jude, two people who got just what they deserved—each other. I hope you'll always be as happy as you are right now."

Jude took Maggie in his arms for another kiss, and Rob drained his glass. He was torn between feeling joy for what they had and pain because the same happiness had been denied him. He tried not to think of Jenny as he watched the couple cut the cake and whirl around the floor for the opening waltz, but he couldn't help picturing the same scene with different players.

Unable to stand it a moment longer, he made a second attempt to slip away.

Maggie's voice stopped him again. "You're next, mister."

Seeing the glint of determination in her eyes, Rob knew he'd already lost. But he had to try, anyway. "Are you sure that's the right order?"

Margret looked toward the refreshment table where Todd, her rambunctious seven-year-old son from a previous marriage, was piling a plate dangerously high with food.

"Well, the *man* who gave me away has his hands full right now. And the only other man I want to dance with seems to have another woman in his arms."

Rob glanced over her shoulder and saw his brother dancing with their mother, Nilda. Her dark Spanish eyes—a feature that both of the Emory brothers had inherited from the Mexican woman—were shining with a mixture of love and happiness.

Even though he and Jude had had different fathers, and Jude was thirty-three to his twenty-four, Rob had always been able to count on his brother to be there for him. He'd been thrilled when Jude and Margret had finally admitted they loved each other. He wanted nothing to cast a pall over their happiness tonight. Especially not his personal problems.

Summoning a smile, Rob took Margret's hand. "Well, then, I'd be honored to dance with you, Maggie. What man in his right mind would pass up the chance to hold you in his arms?"

Margret looked up at him reproachfully as they began to move to the music. "If you think that you're going to distract me with those big brown eyes and that pearly white smile, forget it. I know something's wrong. Now what gives?"

It was Rob's turn to be exasperated. "You never give up, do you?"

"That's how I snared that cagey brother of yours! But seriously, Rob, I want to help. If it hadn't been for you, Jude and I might not be together now."

Rob remembered how he'd served as Margret's confidant and protector after she and her son, Todd, had arrived on the Double Diamond. She'd been truly alone in the world, a widow whose only asset was the Double Diamond—the ranch she'd inherited from her deceased employer, Jude's natural father.

Jude, embittered and weighed down with guilt over the deaths of his first wife and their unborn child, had considered the Double Diamond rightfully his. He had fought Margret every step of the way. And he'd fought the attraction he'd felt toward the woman whose beauty had only reminded him of the ugliness of his emotional and physical scars. But their love had triumphed in the end.

Unlike his own, Rob thought sadly.

With a sigh, he gave in to Margret's gentle persistence. "The woman you saw me talking to was Jenny Landon. She was the one who called me from school in College Station a few weeks ago."

"The one who told you she was breaking your engagement and didn't even have the consideration to give you a reason?" Margret's eyes widened, then narrowed to slits. "How dare she come to my wedding and upset you!"

Rob couldn't help but smile as he saw gentle Margret transform into a growling lioness, ready to do battle in his behalf. "It's all right," he soothed. "Her daddy owns one of the ranches that borders ours. The Emorys and the Landons have been friends for years. I expected Jenny to show up here."

"But something else happened. Something you didn't expect?"

"Even though I was angry and upset about that phone call, I guess I thought that it was just a case of cold feet. That if I gave Jenny enough time, she'd calm down. She'd come to me and say she'd been wrong."

His feet continued to move to the music even though his mind was elsewhere. "When I saw her standing there, I thought that was what had happened. I thought she'd changed her mind. She was looking at me just the way she used to. As if she wanted me, as if she cared about me. And then Sybil Perry came up and started admiring the engagement ring on Jenny's finger. A ring some other man put there. A ring that was more expensive than any *I* could afford."

He gave Margret a self-deprecating smile. "It just goes to show that we all see just what we want to see. She doesn't care about me at all."

Margret looked thoughtful, as if she were remembering the scene that had transpired between Jenny and Rob. "I wouldn't be so sure."

Before Rob could respond to that surprising observation, his brother was tapping him on the shoulder. "My turn, little brother."

Rob yielded with good grace, twirling Margret around and handing her over to Jude without missing a beat.

"But, Rob..." Margret protested, obviously not finished dispensing sisterly advice.

Rob patted her shoulder. "Don't worry about me, Maggie. I'm a big boy. This is your wedding reception. Enjoy yourself."

As Jude whirled her away, her forehead was still creased with a worried frown. Then the frown vanished under the pressure of Jude's lips, and Margret smiled as all of her attention focused on the man she so obviously loved.

Rob stared after them with affection and more than a little wonder. They were as different as night and day in appearance, but they were so much in love. His thoughts turned inevitably to Jenny, but he forced her out of his mind. He'd never had to chase any woman before, and he'd be damned if he'd start with one who clearly didn't want him. And he'd be damned if he'd miss his only brother's wedding reception just to avoid her.

Snagging the first unattached woman he came across, Rob swung back onto the dance floor. He smiled down at his partner, but he found that no matter how studiously he avoided looking in Jenny's direction, it was still her face that lingered in his mind's eye.

The long, shapely leg exposed by the lifted hem of the wedding dress made Rob agree with the half-whispered comments he heard coming from the men around him. Jude Emory sure was a lucky man.

Having fortified himself with three more glasses of champagne, Rob had yielded to Maggie's pleas. He stood with several other reluctant bachelors waiting for the garter to be tossed. He knew only one thing— he wasn't raising his hand or moving an inch. It would have been different if Jenny... With a shake of his head, Rob drove the thought away.

There was a murmur of expectation, then shrieks from the ladies and shouted advice from the gents. Men fell away from Rob left and right, and he felt a soft impact as something landed on his right shoul-

der. Instinctively, he reached for it and came away
with a handful of lace and satin.

Holding the garter up in front of his face, he stared
at the offending item in disbelief. There was laughter
and backslapping all around as the other bachelors
expressed their relief and condolences.

Rob looked at his brother reproachfully. Jude responded with a whoop of laughter and an open invitation. "Come and get him, ladies. He's all yours!"

Giving his brother an I-owe-you-one glare, Rob
slipped the offending garter into his jacket pocket.
Only a few weeks ago he would have been wearing it
proudly on his sleeve, looking forward to the ceremony that would end his bachelor days. Now he didn't
want any part of what it represented.

Still, he couldn't seem to keep himself from searching out Jenny in the much more eager group that had
assembled to catch the bridal bouquet. He saw her
being pushed into line by an insistent Sybil Perry, and
then the bouquet was in the air. As if guided by ra-
dar—or Margret's matchmaking instincts—it came
down directly into Jenny's waiting hands.

There were whistles and applause as the ranch hands
behind Rob began pushing him forward. He saw what
was coming, but there was no graceful way to avoid it.
In an instant, he was face-to-face with Jenny. He had
a choice of completing the traditional dance or caus-
ing a scene at his brother's wedding reception. Which
meant he really had no choice at all.

Carefully, as if she were a pane of glass that might
shatter and cut him at any moment, Rob rested one
hand on her waist. Then he linked the fingers of his
left hand with hers. Two hot, slightly damp palms

came together, and Rob could feel her heart pounding just as fast as his.

He guided her out onto the dance floor, fighting against the knowledge that no other woman would ever feel as right in his arms as this one did.

"Jenny," he whispered, "look at me."

He felt a shiver pass through her and, for a second, he thought she'd refuse. Then, slowly, she turned her head and met his gaze. The breath he hadn't realized he'd been holding came out in a sigh. Suddenly he knew that whatever she felt for the man whose ring she wore, her feelings for him were far from dead.

"Jenny, why? Just tell me why."

Jenny's throat convulsed as she swallowed, and she lowered her lids to shield her eyes from his gaze once more. She didn't want to say the words, the cruel words that she'd rehearsed so many times in her mind. But she had to.

"I—I found a man who had more to offer me than you could."

Something inside Rob turned hard and cold. He had always accepted himself for what he was. He had done well enough in school, had even tried college for a semester. But, in the end, he'd decided against it.

He was already living where he wanted to live, already doing just what he wanted to do. He'd never thought much about his lack of material possessions. Until now.

"More to offer?" he said, hearing the unfamiliar anger and bitterness in his own voice, and not caring. "You mean, it's smarter to marry some rich college boy than to tie yourself to some no-future ranch foreman like me?"

Jenny felt her cheeks flush an even brighter shade of red. She knew she ought to drive the barb in deeper, end it quickly, cleanly. But she couldn't do it. Not when she could feel his pain as surely as she felt her own.

"I wouldn't put it in those terms, Rob."

Hearing the tremor in Jenny's voice, Rob felt something close to satisfaction. "You wouldn't? Well, then, maybe you were talking about some other area of our relationship."

Deliberately, he put his arm around her slender waist and pulled her close to him, tight against the need that she'd aroused in him. The need that he'd never been able to fully control.

Jenny's gaze snapped to his and she caught her breath. She felt the bridal bouquet slip from her fingers and heard it hit the floor behind Rob with a dull thud.

She knew she ought to express outrage and revulsion. She knew she ought to move away. But pretense was beyond her at this time. Now there was only Rob and the honesty of her feelings for him.

Unable to stop herself, she reached up to caress the nape of his neck with one trembling hand.

"Rob," she whispered, infusing that one syllable with all the longing in her heart, all the caring she needed to express, but couldn't.

"The dance is over, *Row-bare-toe*."

Rob looked up from the tantalizing vision of Jenny's lips, a dull flush of anger spreading over his cheeks at the exaggerated pronunciation of the Spanish version of his name. There was only one man in the vicinity of Layton City and the surrounding ranches who had ever taunted him and his brother about the Mexican blood they'd inherited through their mother.

Reluctantly releasing Jenny, Rob turned to face Jack Keel with a contemptuous smile. "Still going in for those unsubtle little digs about my Mexican heritage, Keel? I thought you'd have realized by now that my brother and I think it's something to be proud of."

Keel struck a match and spoke around the fat cigar jutting out between his large, white teeth. "It figures you'd feel that way, *Row-bare-toe.* You never were too bright."

"What do you consider bright?" Rob snapped, his anger and frustration finding an outlet at last. "Moving to Houston and getting richer by the day cheating honest folks out of their hard-earned money? I think I'd rather stay an ignorant old country boy like your daddy. He was a good rancher—and a good neighbor."

Keel's eyes narrowed in obvious surprise and anger. "I thought your brother, Jude, was the one with the temper, boy."

Rob had always been the easygoing Emory, the one who smoothed things over and talked other men out of fighting. But tonight he wasn't backing away from any man.

"You ought to know about Jude's temper, Keel. He beat the living hell out of you when you two were back in high school, didn't he? But I guess you were just too dense to learn from that experience."

The older man's face flushed and he took a step toward Rob.

Rob tensed in anticipation of the first punch. But instead of launching an attack, Keel shouted one word. "Travis!"

A six-and-a-half-foot giant came forward, wiping a trace of frosting from his beard with a small pink napkin. "Yes, Mr. Keel?"

"Get this man away from me."

Before the bodyguard could move, Jenny stepped in front of Keel and pressed a restraining hand against the vest of his expensive, three-piece suit. "Jack, please!"

Covering her hand with his, Keel gave her an indulgent smile. "All right, Travis, back off. I'll let it go this time, Jenny, but only because you asked me to." He turned his gaze to Rob, his words gloating and deliberate. "I may have spent the first half of the evening outside talking over old times with the boys, but I intend to spend the rest of it in here dancing with my fiancée."

Rob looked from the diamond on Jenny's hand to the smug expression on Keel's broad features and the realization surged through him like an electric shock.

"Him?" he said, his gaze pinning Jenny in place as effectively as any physical restraint. "You're marrying *him?*"

The sounds of music and laughter seemed to fade into the distance as Jenny forced herself to meet Rob's accusing gaze, forced herself to give him the only answer she could. "Yes. I'm marrying Jack a week from today. And, after the wedding, we'll be living in Houston."

Keel draped one beefy arm around her shoulders, and Jenny started in reaction. She willed herself not to fight the pressure he exerted as he drew her close against his side.

Rob's image blurring through the tears standing in her eyes, she forced a smile.

Rob struggled to overcome the hurt and the anger, struggled to comprehend what was happening. "You just graduated from veterinary college," he heard himself saying. "You were going to take over Dr. Meyer's practice, to work with horses and cattle. I can't picture you prescribing tranquilizers for somebody's lapdog in Houston."

Jenny tried to think of a response, but in the end it was Keel who answered. "She won't have to work at all now that she's found a man who can give her anything her little heart desires. She's gonna stay home and just mind the babies."

A steel band constricted Rob's chest. He tried once more to make sense out of something that violated every truth he thought he'd known about Jenny Landon.

"Jenny, you've worked toward being a veterinarian ever since you were a little girl. It's a part of who you are, what you are."

Taking a deep breath, Jenny forced herself to finish what she'd begun, to say the things she had to say. The things that would make Rob turn his back on her once and for all so that he could go on with his life. A life that wouldn't include her.

"Being a vet is part of who I *was*. It just isn't important to me anymore. Jack introduced me to a better way of life. A life filled with fine things and cultured people. He's wealthy enough to give me and my children that kind of life. I'd be a fool to pass all that up for what you have to offer."

She stopped talking, unable to force any more lies past the lump in her throat. She felt a kind of cold horror at what she'd just done, and her breaking heart threatened to snap in two at the loathing she saw in Rob's eyes.

Keel laughed and pulled her even closer. Taking the cigar out of his mouth, he waved it in the air to attract attention. "Listen up, everybody! Listen up now!"

The musicians stopped playing and the room gradually quieted as the crowd became aware that Keel had an announcement to make.

"For those of you who haven't heard it yet, Jenny Landon and I are getting married a week from today. That's Saturday morning at the Landon Ranch. I expect all of y'all to be there."

Rob felt gazes boring into the back of his head as everyone who knew about him and Jenny waited for his reaction. When he remained silent and unmoving, a polite ripple of applause gradually began to spread throughout the room.

Keel beamed, obviously pleased with the response. He gave a final wave, then bent his head and covered Jenny's unresisting lips with his own.

Rage filled Rob. A rage so all-consuming and so intense that he knew he had to leave the room. If he didn't, Jack Keel was a dead man, bodyguard or no bodyguard.

Blindly pushing through the still-applauding crowd, he made his way to the dining room. From there he went on to the kitchen, then slipped out the back door into the darkened ranch yard.

His hands shaking, he took deep breaths of cool night air, willing himself to relax, willing away the red mist of anger that was still hovering in front of his eyes. But he couldn't dispel the overwhelming sense of hurt he felt at Jenny's betrayal.

Ever since Jenny had called him to break off their relationship, he'd been aching to go to her, to try to work things out. In the end, he'd managed to restrain himself, waiting for her to come home, hoping she'd approach him first. He ought to thank God that he hadn't gone chasing after her—that he'd saved at least that much wear on his pride. But, instead, he found himself wondering if going to her would have made any difference in what had happened tonight.

Seconds passed and became minutes, minutes ticked by, but Rob still stood in the ranch yard, his emotions raging out of control, his thoughts going around in circles.

"Hey, *hermano,* everyone's gone home. You gonna stay out here all night?"

Rob tensed at the sound of his brother's voice, resenting the intrusion no matter how well-intentioned. "Maybe," he said through gritted teeth. "Maybe I'll do just that."

Jude moved up to stand beside him, his face a shadow in the darkness. "Maggie told me about you and Jenny. I guess I've been so wrapped up in my own problems these past few weeks that I didn't even notice you were having problems of your own."

"Try 'years,'" Rob snapped, needing some outlet for his anger.

"What?"

"You've been wrapped up in your own problems for years!"

Jude's chuckle raised Rob's temper another notch. "I guess you're right about that. I was one bitter, angry hombre—until my happy-go-lucky little brother gave me hell and told me it was high time I stopped feeling sorry for myself."

Rob squeezed his eyes shut and exhaled, letting most of his anger out with the breath. "And you thought it was time to return the favor?"

He felt rather than saw his brother's smile. "Yup. Guess you realize now that it isn't always easy to be a ray of sunshine when you feel like someone's trampled your heart."

Rob felt his face redden and was glad of the darkness. He was about to offer his brother an apology, but Jude spoke first.

"I deserved everything you said to me and then some. If you hadn't helped get me back on track, I probably wouldn't be standing here wearing this godawful rented tuxedo tonight."

Smiling despite himself, Rob turned into his brother's hug.

"Is there anything I can do to help?" Jude asked him as they stepped apart.

Rob started to tell his brother the things Jenny had said, but his attention was distracted by the light that winked on in the window of Jude's bedroom. He thought about the night ahead and about the weeklong honeymoon that his brother would be leaving on early in the morning and shook his head.

"There's nothing you can do for me, Jude. Just see to Maggie. Take care of her."

Jude looked toward the bedroom window and loosened his tie. "Oh, I intend to, little brother. I surely do intend to."

Rob watched as his brother disappeared into the ranch house, then turned to gaze up at the stars. He suddenly felt very much alone. Or maybe lonely was a better word. He hadn't realized how big a part of his hopes and dreams Jenny had owned. Now, suddenly, his future seemed empty without her.

He still felt anger, but there was also an aching sadness—and a growing feeling of puzzlement. He'd known Jenny since she was a child. They'd been neighbors and the same age. They'd gone through school together. She'd been a friend for years before she'd been his sweetheart.

The Jenny he knew didn't think material things were that important. College and a career as a veterinarian had meant everything to her. Now she was acting like she didn't care about that at all.

She said it was over between them, but she still responded to his touch. And was it wishful thinking on his part, or had she actually seemed repelled by Keel's attentions?

The Jenny he knew might have changed her mind about marrying him, but she would never have replaced him with a man like Keel. And she would never have been cruel enough to say the things she'd said to him tonight—even if they were true.

It all added up to one very big puzzle, and he had only a week to solve it. A week before he lost Jenny to Keel forever. Obviously he didn't have any time to waste.

Leaving the stars to their own devices, Rob strode out into the darkness.

Chapter Two

"I said *no!*"

Jenny wrenched open the passenger door and tumbled out of Keel's big, overpriced car. She managed to get her feet under her at the last second, preventing a fall that would have bruised her fast-eroding dignity as well as sundry parts of her anatomy.

Raising her chin, she backed toward the ranch house where her father was—hopefully—still sleeping, oblivious to the drama being enacted in his front yard.

"Come back here, you little chili pepper!"

At the sound of Keel's voice, still husky with a passion she'd tried her best not to arouse, Jenny's stomach threatened to expel the little she'd managed to eat at the reception.

She swallowed hard, fighting against the nausea. "Jack," she began, despising herself for the quaver in her voice, "you know you agreed to wait until after we were married."

"Just because I agreed not to finish the dinner, doesn't mean I'm not entitled to a little nibble or two every now and then."

Jenny felt a wave of revulsion accompanied by an unwise flare of temper. "You're not entitled to anything until we're legally married, Jack Keel. And don't you forget that!"

To Jenny's surprise and frustration, she was answered by a wave of approving masculine laughter. "My father was right about you, angel. You're the nicest girl ever born around these parts. You were still in pigtails when I went away to college, but my daddy's letters were always full of you. 'Jenny Landon's calf won the 4-H competition.... Jenny Landon made valedictorian.' No matter how much money I made in business, he was always disappointed in me. But he thought you were the brightest, prettiest, sweetest thing he'd ever seen. You didn't know he had you all picked out to be the mother of his grandchildren, did you?"

Jenny was at a loss for words. She remembered Frank Keel clearly. He'd been her father's neighbor and friend. A man who had been as humble and kind as his son was egotistical and arrogant. "He's dead, Jack. Surely you're not going through all this for his sake?"

Jack's voice hardened perceptibly, but it was the only sign he gave of having heard her. "I thought that for once, I had a chance of living up to his expectations. I drove all the way from Houston to College Station just to ask you out. The pretty, desirable woman I found there was nothing like the little girl I remembered."

Unused to thinking of herself in those terms, Jenny made a soft sound of disbelief. Keel qualified his statement as he continued his monologue.

"Oh, you weren't as glamorous and sophisticated as the ladies I knew in Houston, but you had ten times their class. In fact, you thought you had too much class for me, didn't you?"

Typically he didn't pause long enough for her to insert an answer. "You turned your little nose up at me as if I was dirt—that time and all the other times I asked. No matter how many flowers I sent, no matter how many gifts I tried to give you, you still wouldn't give me the time of day. Me, Jack Keel!"

For the first time, he had stated a truth that Jenny had suspected from the beginning. "I *thought* that's what you found so attractive about me! You just want to get your revenge for all those times I rejected you. You want to conquer some imagined challenge to your masculine ego. But isn't marriage taking things a little too far?"

She held her breath, waiting for his reply, hoping he'd discuss his reasons with her—something he'd always refused to do before. Hoping that she could somehow persuade him to change his mind. Just when she was beginning to doubt that he'd respond at all, he gave her an answer.

"The more you pushed me away, the more I wanted you. That's true. But somewhere along the way, I came around to seeing my daddy's point of view. I started to want you for my wife. I started to care about you."

Jenny felt her mouth drop open in astonishment. "You can't be serious! If you cared for me, you wouldn't have threatened and coerced me without the slightest consideration for my feelings. I'm nothing to you but another business deal, an objective to be conquered by any means, fair or foul. Well, caring isn't manipulative and selfish. Your father understood that. He would never have approved of you forcing me into marriage.''

Jenny was prepared for denial, for ridicule, for anything but his snort of amusement. ''Don't be so naive, sugarplum. There are as many kinds of caring as there are people. You're right about my daddy, though—he would have taken a horsewhip to me. I loved him, but I never understood him, any more than he understood me. Now, like you said, he's dead. It's me you have to deal with. And you can bet that *my* kind of caring isn't ever going to involve being stupid enough to give up something I want. I wanted you. I went after you. Now I have you. Because I care about you and respect you, I'm giving you until Saturday to get used to that idea.''

Even as Jenny tried to think of how to respond to Keel's chilling, egotistical statement, he pointed one long finger at her and issued a warning. ''After the marriage ceremony's over, there won't be any more holding back, whining or excuses. You'll be mine then, princess. All mine. Just don't *you* forget that.''

Leaving the words lingering behind him like the remnants of a bad dream, Keel gunned the engine and pulled away in a cloud of dust.

Sick at heart, Jenny turned and stumbled in the direction of the ranch house. She had no idea where she would find the courage to go through with her marriage to Jack. Her confrontation with Rob tonight at the wedding reception had all but undone her resolve.

As she opened the front door and stepped into the house, she remembered the hurt in Rob's eyes. She hadn't wanted to hurt him, but she'd had no other choice. Jack had insisted that they go to Jude's wedding. He'd demanded that tonight be the night that they announced their own wedding plans. She'd held off for as long as she could. But now, with her diploma in hand and the wedding only a week away, she'd run out of both time and excuses.

When she'd called Rob from college three weeks ago, it had been in response to Jack's demand. He'd been present, listening to every word. He'd wanted her to tell Rob about their upcoming marriage then. She'd managed to convince him to let her break the news in stages, that there'd be less resistance from Rob that way. In her heart, she'd been hoping that a miracle would happen. That she'd never have to tell Rob about Jack. But tonight had come, and there had been no miracle to save her.

Tonight she'd had to say hurtful things to convince Rob that it was really over between them. Just as she *had* to go through with her marriage to Jack on Saturday, no matter how much she hated the thought.

Jenny blinked away her tears and forcefully banished Rob from her thoughts. Pushing the door shut, she focused on the dimly lit living room. A smile touched her lips—a smile that was equal parts love and exasperation. Her father was sitting up in the old rocking chair, sound asleep.

She let her gaze trail over the dear, familiar face illuminated by the flickering light of the static-filled television screen. Tate Landon had turned sixty-one last August, but he looked older. A lifetime of working outdoors had eroded his features with a network of fine lines. Lines that seemed to Jenny to grow deeper every day.

She tried to think what her life might have been like without this man's protection and care. She couldn't even begin to imagine it.

He had married her mother, Mary, when Jenny was only a few days old, and raised her as his own. And he'd been both mother and father to her after Mary and the baby she'd been carrying had died in child-birth over fifteen years ago.

Somehow, Tate had found the time to dry her tears and to go to PTA meetings. He'd taught her how to ride—and how to cook. From her earliest memory he had loved her, and he had kept her safe.

Jenny felt her faltering resolve strengthen once more as she moved into the room. She placed Margret's wedding bouquet on top of the coffee table and switched off the TV. Then she bent down and kissed her father's tanned, wrinkled brow.

Tate stirred at her touch. He blinked up at her owl-ishly as she removed his reading glasses from their perch on the balding top of his head and slipped them into their case in the breast pocket of his faded bath-robe.

"You shouldn't have waited up for me," Jenny told him in a voice too full of love to be reproachful. "Dr. Hooper says you need your rest."

Tate muttered a few choice words in an undertone too low for Jenny to catch before launching into his standard tirade. "Bossy old quack! As if eight hours of sleep every night is gonna cure what ails me."

Jenny moved his slippers into range of his questing toes, then, biting her lip, stood by as Tate struggled to push himself to his feet. He swayed slightly as he stood upright, and Jenny reached out to steady him.

Pushing her hand aside gently but firmly, he tucked the newspaper he'd been holding under his arm and started down the hall. "I'm not an invalid yet, girl."

"I know that, Daddy," Jenny said automatically.

She trailed after him, hovering like a mother hen. She knew he detested that behavior, but she couldn't seem to help herself. "I wish you had come to the wedding," she said conversationally. "Jude's wife is so beautiful, and everyone was asking after you."

Jenny expected anything except the reply she got.

"I couldn't for shame to show my face at Jude Emory's wedding. Not after the way you've treated Rob."

Staring at her father's flannel-clad back, Jenny felt as if he'd slapped her. He rarely criticized her for any reason and the hurt of it cut her to the bone. She wanted to plead for understanding, to explain why she'd had to jilt Rob. But that was the one thing she could never do.

Taking a deep breath to calm herself, Jenny tried to change the subject. "Did you remember to take your heart pill, Daddy?"

"No, I didn't. I intended to take it, but I fell asleep."

Jenny sighed in exasperation. "The doctor said that if you don't take care of yourself, you could have another heart attack. And the next one could be the last one."

Tate snorted derisively and turned to face her. "If you mention the word doctor one more time..."

Jenny's voice fell to an unsteady whisper. "I just don't want to lose you, Daddy."

Making a great production of the process, Tate took the medicine bottle out of his pocket, snapped the lid open, and swallowed a pill. "There you go. Now if I up and die during the night, you have no one to blame but that damned Dr. Hooper."

"A heart attack is nothing to joke about!"

"Your upcoming marriage to that no-good Jack Keel is enough to give any father a heart attack."

Jenny's face went pale and words failed her. She could only shake her head in denial.

Her father reached out and put a hand on her arm. "You can't be serious about marrying that man. Tell me why you're doing this."

She longed to tell him, to share the terrible secret that she'd kept to herself for far too long. But she didn't dare. She could only fall back on the lie she'd rehearsed. The lie she'd told Rob. "We've already been through this, Daddy. Jack's so much more mature, so much more successful than Rob."

Her father's hand slid away as she raised her eyes to meet his anger-filled gaze.

"You can disguise it with all the fancy words you want, Jenny Landon. But I never thought I'd live to see the day when a daughter of mine would sell herself to the highest bidder. All your life I've been proud of you. But tonight I'm not proud any more. I'm ashamed."

He turned away from her and went into his room. The door slammed shut behind him.

"Daddy..." Jenny wrapped her arms around her middle and turned her face toward the wall. She'd known that the path she had chosen wouldn't be an easy one. She'd known there would be pain, but she hadn't thought her own father would turn against her.

Forcing herself to keep functioning, she continued down the hall and entered the bedroom that had been hers since she was a child. This room had always been a sanctuary, a haven. Now there was nowhere that she could go, nowhere that she could hide.

She closed the door behind her more forcefully than necessary and began to undress in the dark.

It was all so unfair! Here she was, sacrificing everything for her father, and he loathed her for it. But she had to keep her secret, to live with the consequences as best she could. Her daddy would come around in time. The alternative was too painful to think about.

Drawn toward the window, she slipped into her long, cotton nightgown and moved across the worn blue carpet. Impulsively she raised the shade and looked out into the night.

It was dark, the moon hidden behind a cloud—just as her secret was hidden and must stay hidden. Suddenly she pulled the shade down, unable to bear it even a moment longer. Looking out into the darkness was like looking into her own future. She loathed Jack Keel. How could she promise to be his wife?

An image of Rob's face formed in her mind. He'd looked so hurt tonight, so angry. She longed to be able to hold him in her arms and tell him it had all been some horrible mistake. But she couldn't hold him. Not now. Not ever again.

She sank to her knees in front of the window, the tears she'd been holding back all night gathering in her eyes as she imagined the days, the years, without Rob's touch, without his caring.

"Oh, Rob," she whispered. "I'm so sorry. So very sorry."

"What is it you're sorry for, Jen?"

Jenny leapt to her feet and staggered back against the dresser. Her eyes frantically searched the darkness and finally succeeded in locating the shadowy figure stretched out on her bed.

Anger, apprehension and joy warred within her, but she tried to keep her tone aloof. "Just what do you think you're doing here, Rob Emory?"

"This isn't the first time I've been in your room—or in your bed."

Jenny blushed as she remembered the times Rob had climbed through her bedroom window to steal midnight kisses and caresses. But all that was in the past. A past that would never be again.

Right now she was angry, angry at his high-handed behavior and at the way he'd forced a confrontation. Angry because he was making her reject him for a second time, and she didn't know if she was capable of it.

She used the anger and frustration she felt to make her words harsh and cold. "Well, it's the last time you'll be here! I happen to be engaged to another man."

Rob's hopes had soared when he'd heard her whispering his name. Now the hostility in her voice was confusing him again. It was becoming an effort to hold on to his own temper.

"Some engagement you have. I rode up just as you were, uh, getting out of Keel's car. From where I was standing, I couldn't hear much, but it looked more like a wrestling match than a love match to me."

"My relationship with Jack is none of your business!"

Rob swung his legs off the bed and came toward her, visions of the past refocusing his anger and turning his voice to liquid seduction in the darkness. "It wasn't ever that way with us. Remember, Jenny?"

Watching him come toward her, she told herself to move, to go to the door, to call her father. Instead she held her place, waiting for him, yearning for his touch with every fiber of her being.

His arms went around her, his mouth caressing her forehead, her eyelids, her cheeks.

The familiar scent of him revived old memories of hot summer nights and even hotter kisses, of passion aroused and never fulfilled. She wanted him to give her that fulfillment. She wanted him to go on holding her forever until she forgot that a man named Jack Keel had ever been born.

But no matter how much she wanted those things, she knew they could never be.

Summoning her last shred of willpower, she put her palms flat against his chest and pushed him away. "Get out, Rob. Get out now."

Rob stumbled back a step, stunned by her sudden rejection. One minute she'd been all warmth and give, the next she was as cold as a Montana winter.

He tried to read her expression in the darkness, but he could see only shadows. His anger came rolling back with a vengeance, making him twice as determined to wrest an explanation from her. "No way, Jenny. I'm not going anywhere until you tell me the real reason you're marrying that creep. You were the first one in your family to go to college. That was important to you—that and going on to become a veterinarian like you've wanted to do ever since you were a little girl. No man's money could make you give up that dream."

Jenny's hands clenched into fists as she listened to him. How long could she go on lying? How long before she broke down and told him the truth? "Why can't you just believe what I tell you, Rob? Why can't you just leave it at that? I've changed. It's that simple."

"No one changes that much, that fast."

Searching frantically for a way to convince Rob, Jenny suddenly found real feelings and resentments she hadn't even recognized before bubbling to the surface. "This is all your fault! We could have been married long before now, but you just couldn't make that commitment!"

Rob frowned, confused by the sudden change of topic. "What are you talking about? We were engaged!"

"Engaged? You never proposed to me. You never gave me a ring!"

Rob thought about it, and was surprised to realize that what she said was true. "We had an understanding that we'd get married right after you graduated from veterinary college."

All the resentment Jenny had left unvoiced over the years came pouring out. "*You* had the understanding. There was no date set, no wedding arrangements made. If I had come home without Jack Keel, you *still* wouldn't be talking marriage."

"The hell you say!"

She drew in a deep breath to shout back at him, but caught herself in time. With visible effort, she reined in her emotions. She couldn't afford to lose control again. It would make her even more vulnerable. She had to end this. Here and now.

"It's too late for accusations and should-have-beens, Rob. It's too late for anything between us. Please, just go. Just leave me alone."

Rob felt like tearing out his hair in frustration. She'd finally hit on something that sounded like the truth—as she saw it—an issue he had some hope of resolving. Then she'd turned around and told him that it didn't matter whether he was ready for an all-out commitment or not. She'd made up her mind. She'd written him off.

"You're saying it's too late for us? No matter how I feel, no matter what I do or say, it's too late?"

Slowly, reluctantly, Jenny forced herself to speak the words. "Yes, that's exactly what I'm saying."

Rob knew that that should have been the end of it. She'd just told him that their relationship wasn't worth the time and trouble to resurrect. And he might have accepted that if it hadn't been for the undercurrents he'd been feeling ever since he'd seen her at the reception. The look in her eyes, the way her body responded to his. The jagged edge her voice had taken on just now when she'd told him to leave. All of it was wrong for someone who had stopped caring.

Unable to break down the barriers between them any other way, Rob took the only approach he could think of. He stepped close and tried to put his arms around her.

But Jenny had other obligations, another love that bound her. She struggled free of his grasp and backed away from him.

"Why won't you just go away?" she whispered, torn between need and fear.

Slowly, inexorably, he closed in on her again. "You don't really want Keel, Jenny. Even if I hadn't seen what happened at the car earlier, I'd have sworn to that. You do want me."

Jenny's back came up against a wall that effectively blocked any further retreat. Unable to escape, she looked up at her tormentor, conflicting emotions surging through her like a tidal wave. She almost hated him at that moment. Hated him for breaking down her resistance and calling forth feelings she'd never confronted before.

A part of her, a part she hadn't wanted to acknowledge, blamed Rob for delaying their marriage and leaving her open to Jack's machinations. A deep, elemental part of her still longed for him to confront Keel, to force the other man to back down.

Now those dark feelings came rushing out to form words. Words that taunted and dared. Words that, once said, could never be called back. "What woman wouldn't want Jack? He's a powerful, successful man. A man who knows what he wants and isn't afraid to take it."

Rob heard her pain, and he heard a resentment he didn't understand. But for the first time he also heard a call to battle, a verbal gauntlet thrown down before him.

He placed his palms flat against the wall on either side of her shoulders and stared down into her shadowed face. "Is that some kind of a challenge, Jenny? Because if it is, I can meet it any time you say the word."

Jenny stood within the prison of his arms, knowing the primitive forces she'd unleashed. A part of her exulted in them, wanted them to triumph. But who would pay the price if they did?

Suddenly terrified of that price, she tried to duck beneath his arm. He grabbed her and pinned her to the wall with the pressure of his body. The heat of him spread through her like a raging inferno, but she fought against being consumed by it. "Let me go, damn you!"

Rob's voice was a husky whisper that held equal parts passion and anger. "When you told me on the phone that you wanted to break things off with me, I felt like coming up to College Station and shaking some sense into you. Maybe I ought to do it now."

On the verge of surrender, Jenny called up her last reserves of resistance, summoning old, painful memories to the surface. She, the ugly duckling, worshiping Rob, the most popular boy in school, from afar. Even after he'd begun to notice her as more than just a friend, she hadn't been able to believe her good fortune. In the deepest, most secret recesses of her heart, she still did not believe. Now that doubt underlined her words.

"You want to shake me, Rob? Why? Because I'm not falling at your feet? You always thought you could get any girl you wanted if you just turned on the charm. Well, not this girl. Not anymore."

"No?" Rob's hands moved to frame her face, holding it still.

Jenny's hands came up to grasp his, the nails set against the tanned flesh that held her prisoner. But she couldn't bring herself to do more than that. She couldn't bring herself to hurt him any more than she had already, no matter what the cost.

His lips claimed hers with a rough hunger that she was determined to resist. She told herself that she could resist him. She must. But she hadn't counted on the answering hunger that welled up within her. The hunger for the touch, taste and feel of him. The hunger that she'd denied for far too long.

His tongue plunged between her parted lips, and she welcomed the invasion, meeting his strokes with a whimper and a bold foray of her own. A groan that was part relief, part arousal, part triumph escaped from Rob's throat as he let his body sink down against hers.

Hands joined palm to palm, fingers intertwined. Then Rob lifted the barrier of their joined hands from between their bodies, pressing them against the wall above her head. His lips left hers to travel to her earlobe where his tongue caressed and teased.

Jenny's head rolled from side to side against the wall and she shivered as his warm breath tickled her senses. She had to put an end to this. She had to, but not now, not yet.

His mouth moved lower, his hot tongue laving the column of her throat, tracing the soft vee of skin left exposed by the gaping neck of her gown.

Breathless with anticipation, she arched upward, baring the rise of her breast to his ministrations.

He took what she offered, licking at her flesh, pushing aside the thin cotton of her nightgown with his face until her erect nipple was totally exposed and vulnerable.

Jenny gasped as he nuzzled softly with his cheek and trembled as the warmth of his tongue caressed. Then he took the tip of her breast into his mouth and her world collapsed inward in a shock of sensation. Liquid heat collected and pooled in the center of her body, and she lifted her hips to the hard male part of him that was pressed so closely against her.

He released her hands, and she buried them in his sleek black hair, straining to draw him closer. His fingers roved over her, relearning the curves and lines of her body, reclaiming her as his alone. Then they raised the long hem of her gown and slipped beneath it to cup her bare bottom, forcing her hips to arch even closer to his hot, throbbing need.

He had little thought beyond that need except for a firm determination to make her his, to take once and for all the part of her body, the part of her heart that she had always denied him. To break the final barrier that separated them.

He was fumbling with the fastener on his pants when a familiar voice froze him in place.

"What's going on in there? Jenny, are you all right, girl?"

With a curse that was equal parts frustration and despair, Rob let Jenny's gown fall back into place and forced himself to step away from her.

The door opened, and the light was switched on. Rob blinked, his eyes protesting the sudden change from dark to bright. When they finally focused, he saw that Tate Landon looked just as confused as he felt.

"What the hell are you doing here, Rob? And what's that you're wearing?"

Being no fool, Rob chose to answer the last question. "It *was* a tuxedo. I, uh, came straight over here from my brother's wedding."

"On horseback?"

Rob nodded a bit sheepishly.

Tate shook his head as if unable to fathom the other man's reasoning. "In a big hurry to see my daughter, were you?"

"Yes, sir."

"Well, that's fine with me. If I'd've known it was you, I wouldn't have interrupted."

Jenny's eyes widened in shock. She couldn't believe she'd heard correctly.

Rob tried to suppress a grin. "I seem to recall that the last time you caught me in here, you threatened me with a shotgun."

Tate nodded an admission. "That was before I knew who she was gonna replace you with."

Jenny's composure returned in a rush and, along with it, her sense of purpose. "That's entirely my business, Daddy. Rob, I'll thank you to leave. Now."

Rob just stared, unable to believe the change in her. Only moments before she'd been almost a part of him. Now she couldn't have been further away. Her withdrawal roused his temper as nothing else could have. The words seemed to jump out of his mouth as if they had a life of their own. "You'd better be sure you mean that, Jenny, because if I leave now, I'm not coming back."

Jenny wanted to beg him to stay. But that wasn't one of her options. Not now. Not ever. "I'm sure. I made my choice the day I accepted Jack's proposal."

Rob's last hope died and anger rose up to take its place. "I hope for your sake, you can live with that choice."

Biting her lip to keep from calling out his name, Jenny watched as he walked past her father and through the bedroom doorway. He didn't look back.

She told herself that she should feel relieved now
that he was finally gone, now that he had finally given
up on them. But all she felt was a vast, yearning emptiness that she doubted would ever be filled.

"Oh, Daddy." She walked over to her father and
put her arms around him. Obviously bewildered, he
refrained from questions and reproaches. Instead he
simply held her close, patted her back consolingly, and
told her that everything was going to be all right.

Jenny silently vowed that somehow, some way, she
would make it all right. Her heart ached for Rob, but
she prayed he would stay away. If he came back, she
didn't know how she would ever find the strength to
say goodbye to him again.

Chapter Three

"Quit bawlin', you old hussy! You're the one who got yourself into this mess."

Rob's words were forced through clenched teeth and followed by a string of obscenities. The runty, old brindle cow was not impressed. She let out another long, plaintive bellow.

Throwing a half hitch over his dally, Rob left his mare to maintain tension on the rope that stretched from the cow's horns to the saddlehorn. He approached the mud hole with grim determination. Cursing all the way, he waded through the muck until he reached the mired cow. Then he bent down and began to dig away the mud around one foreleg, trying to free it from the grip of the ooze.

"Help me, damn it! You may want to stay in here, but I sure as hell don't."

The cow rolled her eyes and bellowed again. Rob

maneuvered around to her back quarters and started on another leg. "Come on, you old bag of bones!"

With no warning, the cow suddenly bounded forward, free of the pull of the mud at last.

Wiping splattered slime from his face with a shirt sleeve, Rob fought his way back onto solid ground. He stood still for a moment, shaking mud from his hands, struggling to catch his breath.

Inevitably, his mind strayed back to the confrontation he'd had with Jenny the night before. He'd thought a lot about the things she'd said, but they still made little sense to him.

One minute they'd been talking about Keel's money and Jenny had been claiming she'd changed. He'd been working on attacking the truth of that assertion when, femalelike, she'd switched topics and tactics and gone on the offensive about his lack of commitment.

Hell, he'd told the woman he was serious about her four years ago. He'd mentioned the future and settling down and all that stuff. She'd been the one to back away, talking about how young they were, how she wanted to finish school first. Now, he was somehow to blame for that. And for dating the women he clearly remembered her telling him he was free to date. Four years was one damned long time. What in the hell did she expect a man to do, take cold showers and pray the need would go away? How could—

The brindle cow, obviously recovered from her ordeal in the mud hole, chose that moment to charge his mare. Brandy dodged, then bucked, allowing both the cow and the rope to pass under her belly. The saddle, with the rope still wrapped around the horn, was jerked around and down until it hung beneath the cow pony.

Watching in disbelief and horror, Rob was torn between the urge to try to rescue the mare and the good sense that warned him to stand clear. Thankfully, the half hitch he'd put in the rope didn't hold, and the wrap was pulled free of the saddlehorn.

Rob breathed an audible sigh of relief.

The cow chose that moment to find herself a new victim. She came charging at him from the far side of the mare. Rob turned around to run and found himself falling face first into the mud.

Seconds later, he lurched to his feet, cursing and sputtering, every inch of his body covered with the sticky muck.

The cow, who had halted at the edge of the mire, eyed him with every evidence of satisfaction. Then she turned her tail to him and loped off across the pasture, trailing his best rope behind her.

Rob tromped out of the hole, squelching mud at every step. His skittish mount snorted at his approach and shied away. He had to spend a half hour sweet-talking her before she finally stood still and allowed him to right the saddle and haul his mud-covered body onto her back.

And it had all happened because he'd let his attention stray from an ornery brindle cow to Jenny Landon.

Damn all females, anyway!

Rob was in a foul mood when he rode into the Double Diamond ranch yard at noontime. He'd washed off the bulk of the mud in the creek, but he knew he was still a sorry sight. The hoots of laughter and the catcalls that greeted him did nothing to improve matters. A few weeks ago he would have been laughing right along with the hands. Now he felt like strangling every fool one of them.

Part of the problem was the way his temper had been rubbed raw by the situation with Jenny. The other part had to do with his brother, Jude, becoming the ranch owner and promoting him to foreman.

He'd been working with the hands since he was a kid. His carefree, easygoing personality had made him the practical joker, the peacemaker, everyone's little brother. Since the death of Ben Emory—his father and Jude's stepdad—Jude had always been the one who gave the orders on the ranch. True, Rob had taken charge of the summertime dude ranch guests, partly because he enjoyed the socializing, but mostly because Jude refused to have anything to do with that part of the business. But when it came to the horses and the cattle, Jude was the boss.

Rob had never before had the reason or the inclination to try to change that. Oh, he worked as hard as the next man and did the job right. But life was too short for the worry and responsibility of bossing a bunch of ornery, independent-minded cowpokes when Jude had always been more than able to handle the task alone.

Lately, though, things had changed. He'd been looking forward to Jenny graduating, looking forward to taking on the responsibility of a wife and family. Somehow, given all that, it had seemed natural for him to step into the job of foreman. So far, the hands hadn't seen it that way.

He'd tried to tread easy, to suggest rather than order. But the hands, used to his being their pal instead of their boss, were going about things their own way. To date, it hadn't amounted to much, so he had let it slide. But he couldn't sit on the fence forever. Something had to give. He just didn't want it to give today—not when he was spoiling for a fight, anyway.

Rob slid to the ground by the main corral. He was wiping his saddle down with an old rag when Will Tavers apparently judged it safe to approach.

Will was a year older than Rob, and, from the time Will's family had first moved down from Oklahoma when Rob was fifteen, they'd been both friends and competitors. Whether it was racing horses and pickups to prove who owned the fastest, downing shooters to see who had the greatest tolerance for tequila, or vying to win the favors of the most desirable girl, Rob and Will had done it all.

Predictably, Will was one of the worst offenders when it came to not taking his orders seriously.

Rob made a real effort to find the patience he seemed to have lost somewhere in the past few days. "How's it going, Will?"

"Fine, Rob. Just fine. Have a little accident, did you?"

Biting back a sarcastic denigration of Will's intelligence and ancestry, Rob forced himself to answer civilly. "Yeah, well that's what happens when you don't keep your mind on the job at hand. And while we're on the subject of work, all that rain we've been having washed out the water gap over by the Landon place. I'd like you to take Jesse and go rebuild it."

Will grimaced. Spending hours knee-deep in water jamming old fence posts into a creek bottom wasn't any cowboy's idea of a good time. "Hell, Rob, it is Sunday, you know."

It had ceased to matter to Rob what day of the week it was. He only knew it was one day closer to Jenny's wedding. "All right, then. Get it done tomorrow."

"Damn it, Rob, all you talk about lately is work. You're getting to sound like an old man. This thing with Jenny sure has taken the starch out of you."

Rob stopped rubbing the saddle and pinned Will with a look. "I'm not any woman's fool."

Will shifted his feet and looked at the ground between his boots. "I said that very thing to old Larry just this morning. He claims he saw you ride out of here last night in your wedding suit, headed toward the Landon spread."

Rob felt his neck turn red, but his gaze never wavered. "I've never had to chase any woman."

"Well, that's what I told Larry. You'd have to be crazy to waste time on Jenny. She was just looking for a meal ticket, and she found a richer one than you. Like I been telling you, you're way too young to be thinking about marriage, anyway. Why tie yourself down to one filly when there's a whole pastureful out there just longing for a man to feed them a little sugar?"

Rob felt his bruised ego begin to respond to Will's flattering comments. "Maybe you're right."

"'Course I am. Why, just this morning when I was in Layton City, one of your old girlfriends was asking after you."

Rob loosened the cinch and pulled the saddle from the mare, pretending indifference. "Who's that?"

Will gave him a sly wink accompanied by a punch in the arm that nearly caused him to drop the saddle. "Lissa Jackson."

"She's a married woman," Rob reminded him. He started for the tack room, Will trailing behind.

"Not anymore. She just got her divorce and she's looking for someone to celebrate with—if you know what I mean."

Rob unloaded the saddle, finding it hard to dredge up any enthusiasm despite the picture Will was working so hard to paint. "So why didn't *you* ask her out?"

"I hinted around it, but it didn't take me long to get the idea that she had her little heart set on you."

Rob was about to shrug off Will's observation when he stopped himself. The more he thought about going out with Lissa again, the more the idea appealed to him. Jenny had been doing her level best to prove that she didn't need him or want him. Lissa was sassy, sexy and easy on the eyes. The fact that she was a friend of Jenny's was the icing on the cake.

"Is Lissa still living in her parents' old house?"

Will let out a whoop of approval and slapped him on the back. "Yes, sir, she is. I'll meet you both at the Busted Flush tonight, and I'll buy the first round. Twenty bucks says that little blond waitress with the bodacious ta-tas lets me take her home."

Rob forced a smile. "Forty says the lady turns you down flat. Again."

He watched Will walk back out into the sunlight and wondered why he suddenly felt so old.

Sitting in his pickup in front of Lissa Jackson's house in Layton City, Rob tried to decide whether to drive away or to get out of the truck. The place looked just the same as it had the last time he'd picked Lissa up for a date when they were both in high school. He tried to generate some enthusiasm for her and for those good old days, but his thoughts kept straying back to Jenny. That, finally, was the deciding factor.

Slamming the door of the pickup behind him, he started up the flower-bordered walkway. He pushed on the rusted doorbell and waited for the chimes. But there was only silence.

"Damned thing still doesn't work," he muttered.

Lissa's daddy never had been one to waste his free time working around the house. Apparently she'd married—and divorced—a man with the same priorities.

Removing the new black Stetson he'd been forced to buy to replace the one the mud had ruined that morning, he knocked on the door. Then he stood on the porch shifting from one foot to the other, wondering if Lissa was even at home.

He'd thought of calling ahead, but had been half afraid he'd make the date and then chicken out at the last minute. He figured that once he actually saw her, he might be able to generate a little interest in taking things further.

"Oh, to hell with it."

Rob was just turning away with something akin to a feeling of relief when the door finally swung open.

"Surprise!" Lissa Jackson and five other familiar female faces were grinning at him as if he were the head judge of some televised beauty pageant. It was hard to say who was truly more surprised, him or them. As he watched, their smiles turned into round *O*s of astonishment, and they stared back at him in obvious disbelief.

Debbie Armbruster, nine months pregnant if she was a day, was the first to find her voice. "Why, you're not Jenny!"

Rob was suddenly reminded why Debbie had graduated at the bottom of their high school class. "I'd say that's a safe bet, sweetheart."

Debbie looked him up and down as if she truly suspected he might be hiding Jenny somewhere on his person. "Well, where is she, then?"

"She's right here."

At the sound of Jenny's voice so close behind him, Rob felt a tingling sensation that seemed to start at the back of his neck and spread like wildfire over the entire surface of his body. He recognized it as anticipation. He told himself that it had nothing to do with desire and everything to do with revenge. No man could have asked for a better opportunity for the latter.

Willing his mouth to smile, he turned and met her gaze. "Surprise, Jen."

Rob rested his left ankle on his right knee, spread his arms out along the back of the sofa, and tried not to look as foolish as he felt. He knew he ought to leave, but there was a heavy knot of anger in his chest that was keeping him anchored firmly in place.

Reaching for the tall, cool lemonade that Lissa was holding out to him, he gave her a smile calculated to melt every ice cube in the glass. "Thank you, darlin'."

Out of the corner of his eye, he saw Jenny tense in her armchair—a real accomplishment considering the fact that she'd been as stiff as a preacher's collar already. He felt a surge of vengeful satisfaction.

Lissa settled to his left, a raised eyebrow giving her words a hint of irony. "Are you enjoying your first wedding shower, Rob?"

Rob's smile shifted from seductive to genuinely amused. He'd almost forgotten that Lissa had a quick wit and a truly wicked sense of humor in addition to her other more obvious charms.

"Of course, I'm enjoying myself. It's every man's fantasy having six lovely ladies all to himself."

Actually, it was pretty damned uncomfortable being in a room with two ex-girlfriends and one ex-fiancée. He only hoped that Jenny was feeling even more ill at ease than he was.

There was a scattering of girlish giggles in response to his comment. Cindy Harper, who was seated on the sofa to his right, batted her false eyelashes at him and patted her puffed-up mass of hair. "Oh, Rob, you are a devil! I really miss those hours we spent lying in that old pickup of yours just admiring the stars."

Before Rob could even think of a response, Lissa chuckled and leaned around him to look at Cindy. "Is that what you were admiring, Cindy Ann?"

Trying his damnedest not to blush, Rob swallowed half a glass of lemonade in one gulp. He focused on Jenny's face, willing her to look at him, willing her to care that Cindy Harper, four years married, mother of three, still found him fascinating.

But Jenny wouldn't meet his gaze. After the storm of emotion Rob had inspired in her during his visit to her bedroom the night before, she was determined to keep her cool today. A repeat of last night's performance would be disastrous. She had to keep her emotions under control no matter how much he tried to provoke her. She had to honor her promise to Jack Keel.

Moving slowly, she bent over and picked up a gift with a hand that shook only slightly.

"Careful now, Jenny," Debbie warned with apparent seriousness. "Remember, every ribbon you break means another baby!"

The bottom seemed to drop out of Rob's stomach at the thought of Jenny having babies that looked like Keel—or any other man for that matter.

Jenny's gaze glanced off his, and he could have sworn she was thinking the same thought. Then she smiled at something Debbie was saying, and Rob felt like a fool. Jenny had made her choice. How long was it going to take him to accept that simple fact?

Deliberately, he let his left arm come down to rest on Lissa's shoulders. He felt the warmth of her bare skin against his palm and his mind registered the pleasant contact. But his attention was focused on Jenny.

He watched as she pulled something black out of a pile of tissue paper and held it up. The material was so thin, he could see her fingers through it.

April Thompson gave a soft, low whistle. "Now, I bet that'll keep Jack up all night!"

The laughter that followed tore across Rob's nerve endings like fingernails across a blackboard. He wanted to jump up and drag Jenny out of the room, to spirit her far away from Layton City and Jack Keel. He wanted to hold her and kiss her and take her until she admitted that she cared for him and him alone.

Instead he sat sipping lemonade with one arm around Lissa, and flirted outrageously with any female who so much as glanced his way. He watched Debbie stapling discarded ribbons and bows on to a paper plate to make an absurd hat for Jenny. He observed Cindy surreptitiously writing down everything Jenny said, and he listened to it all being read back to more laughter. He smiled for the photos that April took to record it all. And he felt Jenny slipping further away from him with every passing minute.

Finally, when he thought he couldn't take another smile, another stupid game, or another bawdy comment, they adjourned to the dining room. There, a yellow-and-white sheet cake covered a good portion of the shiny mahogany table. Jenny cut the first slice to enthusiastic applause. Another flashbulb died.

Lissa slipped an arm around his waist and smiled up at him. "The coffee should be just about ready. Would you bring it out for me?"

"Anything your little heart desires, ma'am." He gave her a wink and a pat on one nicely curved hip as he walked through the swinging door that led to the kitchen.

Alone in the quiet room, he moved to the sink, braced a palm on either side, and let his head hang. He felt as if he'd been thrown high and stomped hard. Why on earth had he been fool enough to stay? To try to hurt Jenny? To show her he didn't care? That wasn't clear thinking and he knew it. If he had any sense left, he'd escape out the kitchen door while he had the chance.

"Robert Emory, what the hell do you think you're doing?"

A genuine smile tugged at the corners of Rob's mouth, and he whispered a silent prayer of thanks. Then he turned around, crossed his arms over his chest, and leaned back against the sink. "I'm getting the coffee, Jen."

Her face was pale except for two bright red spots high on her cheeks and, as she came closer, he could see the pulse beating in her throat. If she'd been a filly, he'd have headed for the corral fence. As it was, he figured he was safe enough. For the moment.

"Don't play dumb with me! How dare you crash my bridal shower?"

"I had no intention of crashing your shower," he told her truthfully. "I was dropping by to see Lissa."

He felt an immense sense of satisfaction as she deflated like a pin-stuck balloon. "You didn't know about the shower?"

"Nope. I was as surprised as you were."

She had turned away, but now she turned back to face him, gathering steam again. "Well, once you realized what it was, you didn't have to stay and act like . . . like a bull in a pastureful of cows!"

Rob had to struggle to keep his smile from breaking into an out-and-out grin. "It was just a little harmless flirting, Jenny. It's not as if I have an understanding with any particular woman."

Jenny saw red. It was hard enough trying to get through a wedding shower that celebrated her marriage to Jack Keel without having Rob there to remind her of what she would never have. And the added strain of watching him act the fool with her friends had brought all her old insecurities rushing back. His comment about "an understanding" was the last straw.

"Would it have mattered to you if we did still have 'an understanding,' Rob? I don't think so. I think you would have acted exactly the same way."

The hurt in her voice wiped the smile from Rob's face. He pushed away from the sink and moved toward her. "You threw that up in my face last night, too. This time, you're not getting away with it. You were the one who said we should wait and date other people. You were the one who wanted to concentrate on finishing school."

"And that was just fine with you. You didn't once push for anything more!"

"Because what you wanted was important to me!"

"Because happy-go-lucky, no-responsibilities-he-can't-shuck-at-a-few-days'-notice Rob would rather play the field than be tied down to some female horse doctor!"

The unfairness of her accusations made him want to shake her. He grabbed her arms and was close to doing just that when he made the mistake of looking into her eyes. Suddenly he was overwhelmed by an emotion just as strong as anger but infinitely softer.

Jenny felt the change in him and it frightened her more than his anger ever could.

"Don't, please!" she whispered, wondering whether she was talking to Rob or to herself.

"Why not? I know you want me."

Jenny knew he wouldn't believe her even if she denied it. Not after last night. Desperately, with the part of her brain that was still capable of functioning, she searched for an explanation, a way out. And one came to her.

"You're right, Rob. I want you. Like all those women from the city who come to spend their vacations at the dude ranch. They're all looking for a sexy, handsome cowboy to show them a good time. But not many would be stupid enough to want to marry one."

Rob froze in place, feeling the impact of her words like a physical blow. Then he saw the pain in her eyes, the hurt that appeared every time she struck out at him. And he knew it wasn't over yet.

"So that's how it is, Jenny? You just want my body. You don't care about me at all?"

"That's how it is," she said, attempting to ease from his grasp.

His arms went around her, and all at once he was holding her so close she could count his heartbeats.

"When did you stop caring?" he asked, his lips caressing her temple.

She shuddered and tried again to push away from him, but he refused to allow it. Her mind whirled under the pressure of conflicting emotions she couldn't hope to deal with. "I—I'm not sure."

He had one hand at her nape now, his lips hovering inches above hers. "Was it when you started to see Keel, Jenny? Was that when it happened?"

"Yes!" Jenny agreed frantically, turning her face away from his questing lips. "Yes, that's it."

"And just when *did* you start seeing him?"

He was as merciless as a defense attorney cross-examining a key witness—and Jenny was fast running out of answers.

"Leave me alone," she said as firmly as she could manage. "I don't have to answer to you!"

"Well, then, let me have the pleasure of speaking for you."

To her astonishment, he let her go. She fell back against the counter and hung there, fighting for breath and control.

Holding her gaze, he drew a dirty, water-stained piece of stationery from his shirt pocket and waved it in front of her face.

"'I miss you so much, Rob,'" he quoted. "'I can't wait until graduation to see you. Can't you come up just for a weekend?' That's what you wrote in this

letter, Jenny. It was postmarked a week before that
Dear John phone call of yours.''

Jenny swallowed hard, feeling like a cornered animal. ''I-it's called hedging your bets.''

Rob's eyes narrowed, and he stepped closer,
crowding her again. ''Meaning you were writing things
like this to me and seeing Keel on the side. Some
women, maybe. But Jenny Landon? The only stu-
dent in Miss Graham's class who didn't cheat on that
midterm? The one who lost her driving privileges for
six months because she told the unvarnished truth
about the dent she put in her daddy's brand-new
truck?''

Jenny wanted nothing more than to confirm Rob's
belief in her, to go into his arms and tell him everything. But the thought of what would follow terrified
her. She had to stop him now, now before he managed to wheedle the truth out of her. But before she
could find the right words, his hands were framing her
face, lifting her gaze to his.

''Jen, I swear, if you try one more time to convince
me that the big, wicked city has changed you, I'll be
tempted to turn you over my knee. I'm just not buying it. You cared about me then and you care about me
now. Hell, you were so jealous a few minutes ago, you
turned four shades of green. Admit it.''

His lips touched hers lightly, his tongue tracing the
outline of her mouth. ''Say it, Jen.''

Jenny's hands clutched at his shirt. She felt like
screaming under the tender torture he was inflicting.
''I can't. I—''

The sound of the kitchen door opening cut her off
in midsentence. She jumped away from Rob, torn between frustration and reproach. How could she have

let things get out of hand again? She was the one playing with fire, but it was someone else who was going to get burned. Someone she had sworn to protect no matter what it cost her.

Debbie moved into the doorway, one hand pressed to her distended abdomen. "Isn't that coffee ready yet?"

"Right here."

Jenny reached for the pot, but Rob put a restraining hand on her arm. "We're not finished."

Jenny forced herself to shake him off and pick up the hot carafe. "Yes, we are."

"You think so?"

"I know so," Jenny told him, trying not to choke on the words. "I'm marrying Keel on Saturday, and that's about as finished as it can get."

Jenny squeezed past Debbie and left the kitchen. Debbie gave Rob a look that was part contempt and part pity before following in Jenny's wake.

Rob watched the connecting door swing slowly back and forth, then turned and aimed a kick at a low-lying cupboard. If that was the way she wanted things, then that was just fine with him. He was sick of pounding his head against a brick wall.

His jaw set, he scooped the letter off the floor and lobbed it into the wastebasket. Then he headed for the dining room and Lissa Jackson.

"Good night, Lissa. Thanks so much for giving me the shower."

Rob watched as Jenny piled the last of her gifts on the back seat of her car. That accomplished, she climbed into the driver's seat and shut the door behind her. Only then did she deign to acknowledge his existence. "Good night, Rob."

Rob put an arm around Lissa's narrow waist and pulled her close against his side. "*Goodbye,* Jenny."

Jenny looked up and felt a sudden, uncharacteristic urge to slap the both of them. Hard. She would have died before giving in to that urge, and, besides, it wouldn't have done one bit of good. Rob wasn't hers anymore. He never really had been.

Deliberately, she averted her gaze and put the car into reverse.

Rob watched her drive away and most of his anger went with her. He fought off the heavy, hopeless feeling that tried to settle in its place. He was glad that she was finally gone. Now he could be alone with a woman who wanted his attentions.

Suddenly he felt a sharp jab in the area of his rib cage.

"Wake up, cowboy!"

"What?" Rob looked down at Lissa, chagrined to find that his thoughts had been so absorbed by Jenny that he hadn't even been listening to the woman standing right next to him.

"I said, are you all filled up with cake and hors d'oeuvres, or do you want something for dinner?"

"Sure I want dinner—that and anything else you're offering."

Lissa gave him a Mona Lisa smile and led him back into the house. "Uh-huh."

She moved away from him to shut the front door, and he let her go without a second thought. "What is 'uh-huh' supposed to mean?"

"It means that I hope you've got fire insurance. That torch you're carrying for Jenny is hot enough to burn this two-bit town to the ground. Not that that's such a bad idea."

Rob followed her into the kitchen and pulled open the refrigerator door for her. "Jenny's marrying Jack Keel in six days."

"Yes, I know that. I just gave her a wedding shower. How about a roast beef sandwich and some home-made potato salad?"

"Sounds good."

He watched as she piled food items onto the counter, and all at once the thought hit him. Women loved to talk to other women about their feelings. Jenny just might have confided in Lissa.

He picked up the bread and the platter of beef and led the way into the dining room. "Did, uh, Jenny ever talk to you about...you know, getting mar-ried?" he asked, straining to sound casual.

Lissa sat down at the dining-room table and started slicing roast beef. "Getting married was always im-portant to Jenny. I guess because her real daddy wasn't married to her mama."

Rob had forgotten that Tate wasn't Jenny's natural father. It was hard for him to imagine anyone other than Tate ever filling that position. Suddenly he was hungry for details about Jenny. Even things that hadn't seemed important enough to ask about be-fore. "I think she told me her real daddy's name was Roy...no, Leroy Parker. And he worked as a hand for Jack Keel's father, didn't he?"

Lissa handed him a plate filled with food, and licked a stray dab of mustard off her finger. "I'm not sure about that part. I remember her telling me that her mama, Mary, fell in love with her real daddy while she was still in high school. She had to drop out 'cause she got pregnant with Jenny. When her own daddy threw her out of the house, Parker promised to marry her. Instead he only took her to live with him. After a while, he turned mean and started to knock her around and all."

"Just where was Tate during all this?"

"Well, Jenny never said. But, according to the way my mama tells it, everyone knew Tate was sweet on Mary. He just didn't speak up because he was almost twenty years older. But I guess after a while he just couldn't stand by and see her abused, no matter what. He ran Leroy Parker off and no one's seen the bastard around here since."

Rob digested the information, trying to think of how to lead up to what he really wanted to ask. But Lissa spoke before he did.

"Look, Rob, I think it would save us both a lot of time if I just came out and told you what you want to know. When Jenny talked about marriage, she was talking about you, not Jack."

Rob hated the little thrill of hope that seemed to come sneaking up on him out of nowhere. He tried to ignore it. "You sure of that?"

"Jack's had the hots for Jenny for years. She always thought he was a creep. I couldn't believe it when she told me she was going to marry him. I still don't understand it. The only thing he's got going for him is money, and Jenny couldn't care less about that."

Rob leaned toward her, his food forgotten. He felt vindicated at last. Lissa was echoing his own gut feelings about Jenny. But that still didn't clear things up. "Jenny did give me another reason for marrying him. Something about being tired of waiting around for me to propose. But that's crazy. She always knew I wanted to marry her.''

"Did she? You're a man who's always accomplished whatever he's set his mind to, Rob. If you'd really wanted to marry her during the last four years, I think you would have done it."

Pushing back in his chair, Rob glared at her. "Don't you start with that, too, Lissa. *She* was the one who put *me* off!"

"And you let her? Just how hard did you fight?"

Rob was about to snap out an answer when, for the first time, he stopped and really thought about that question. He *had* wanted Jenny to agree to marriage. Failing that, he had at least wanted to get her into bed. When she'd turned him down on both counts, he'd blustered a bit, but he hadn't exactly tried to force the issue.

He'd told himself at the time that he was being generous and unselfish. But had that really been the case? He'd known Jenny, and he'd known that she wasn't going to be sleeping with anyone else. He'd had no doubt that they'd be married when she was through with veterinary college. In the meantime, he'd been only twenty years old and life was still an adventure. He was happy with his work and his family. Women, as always, were available. He'd told himself that it had been Jenny's decision to limit their relationship and to keep dating others, and that four years was a long time to wait.

Even when they'd seen each other during vacations and summers at home, he'd been a little frustrated but generally comfortable with the relationship. Yet, as time had passed, he'd begun to look forward more and more to settling down and sharing a future with Jenny.

Hell, for the past few months, he'd actually been day-dreaming about what it would be like to be a husband—and maybe even a daddy. At least, he'd been dreaming of it until Jenny had called him from college to say goodbye and good riddance.

He felt a touch on his arm and looked up to meet Lissa's level gaze. "I'll say this so that even a man can understand it, Rob. Jenny thought that you still had some growing up to do. That you needed time and space to kick up your heels. So she let you run as far and as fast as you wanted to. She was sure that you'd get tired of all that running if she waited long enough. She thought that, when you were ready, the right woman would have no trouble settling you down. And she was sure she was the right woman."

Rob wasn't quite sure whether he ought to be indignant or grateful for Lissa's frankness. "If all that's true, then why in the hell is she marrying Keel?"

"I don't know. But I do know that you're more interested in talking about Jenny than you'll ever be in getting it on with me—or in finishing that sandwich. So, if you're done with your questions, I'd like to take a shower and get some sleep."

Rob gazed at her with growing admiration. "You're so damned honest, Lissa. You make it hard for me to be anything but the same—with you and with myself. I did come over here to ask you out, but only because I was angry with Jenny. You deserve a lot better than that. I'm sorry."

She linked her arm through his and they walked to the door together. "No hard feelings. Something told me I didn't have a chance with you, but with Jenny getting married—" she shrugged "—I figured it was worth a shot. Good night, Rob."

Pulling his Stetson into place, he kissed her lightly. "That ex-husband of yours was a fool, honey."

She grinned and patted his arm. "Don't I know it. You take care, y'hear?"

His hand was on the door of his pickup when she called after him. "I think Jenny still cares about you, Rob. I don't know why she's acting the way she is, but I don't think you should give up on her yet."

"Thanks, Lissa. Thanks for everything."

"Any time. And, Rob..."

"Yeah?"

"You be sure and give me a call if you're ever really free."

Rob was already on the road when Lissa's words finally penetrated. Would he ever really be free of Jenny? He was just beginning to understand that all these years he'd been sitting back, taking their relationship for granted. It was only now that he was about to lose her for good that he knew just how much he cared—and just how much it was going to hurt if he didn't manage to win her back. He not only cared about her, he *needed* her.

Rob stared into the darkness and realized that he'd finally come face-to-face with the truth, and he didn't like what he was seeing. Not one little bit.

Chapter Four

Jenny stood impatiently as the seamstress adjusted and pinned her wedding dress, her eyes avoiding the fitting room mirror. When she had pictured Rob in the role of the groom, she had imagined that getting married would be the happiest event of her life. Now that she was marrying Jack Keel those hopes and fantasies seemed like something that had belonged to another person, another lifetime.

After what had happened at the shower yesterday, she would be lucky if Rob didn't cross the street every time he saw her coming. Or maybe she would never see him again at all.

The nearby ranch Jack had inherited from his recently deceased father was no more than a showplace now. After the wedding, Jack expected her to live with him in Houston. Not only was she being torn away from Rob, but from her father, her friends, and the career she'd dreamed all her life of pursuing.

"Please try to relax, Miss Landon," the elderly seamstress pleaded. "You're so tense, I can't get this last pin in."

Jenny took a deep breath then released it, making a conscious effort to rid herself of a tension that seemed to be with her even when she slept.

"There. All finished. Isn't it lovely?"

Jenny glanced into the mirror and saw only emptiness and pain. She gave the woman the best smile she could manage. "You do beautiful work."

The seamstress beamed at her, and Jenny felt the day hadn't been a total loss.

She glanced at her watch as she slipped into her street clothes. Jack had dropped her off at the mall in San Antonio only half an hour ago. She still had an hour before he was supposed to come back to get her. An hour of unexpected freedom. It was something she would have taken for granted just weeks ago. Now it was a luxury she intended to take full advantage of.

Stepping out of the bridal shop into the crowded mall, she looked right and left, trying to decide where to go first. Then the pet store across the way caught her eye, and she was lost.

Walking over to the window, she saw a purebred German shepherd puppy lying in a display enclosure that had been lined with shredded newspaper. At first glance he looked healthy, but she wondered if that were really the case. Some pet stores were notorious for their mistreatment of animals.

She tapped on the glass and the animal's ears sprang to attention. He hopped up and placed his forepaws on the glass, trying to lick her hand.

"Sure wish *I* had a puppy like that."

Jenny looked down to see a pair of heart-stopping green eyes peering up at her from beneath a fringe of blond bangs. The little boy's delicate features were an almost startling contrast to his very masculine costume of miniature Stetson, jeans and Western boots. The unselfconscious pose he struck, thumbs hooked into belt loops, one knee bent and thrust forward, brought a smile to her lips. He was a cowboy in the making if she'd ever seen one.

"He's a beauty, all right," she said, seconding his approval of the puppy. "Won't your mama and daddy let you get a dog?"

The gleam in the little boy's eyes dimmed a bit, and the corners of his mouth dipped down. "They went away."

Jenny's own smile was fading rapidly. The child certainly didn't appear neglected. "They must have asked someone to take care of you while they were gone," she prompted, just to make sure.

"You must mean me."

At the sound of the familiar voice, Jenny automatically looked up. She saw Rob's reflection behind her own in the pet store window and her heart went into overdrive.

She had spent a nearly sleepless night tossing and turning, picturing Rob and Lissa together. She'd alternated between jealousy, anger and despair until she'd mercifully fallen into a troubled sleep shortly before dawn.

Now, here he was again. Despite the episode with Lissa, she would have welcomed him with open arms if she could. But that wasn't possible. So there would be more fighting, more hurting, and she wasn't sure how much more she could stand. Warily, she turned to face him.

Smiling at her, he moved to put his hand on the little boy's shoulder. "Jenny Landon, I'd like you to meet Todd Brolin—soon to be Todd Emory once the paperwork goes through. Todd is Maggie's son from her first marriage."

He gazed down into the face that was now upturned and grinning. "Todd has been feeling a little down since his mama and his new daddy left him to go away for their honeymoon. So I brought him in to San Antonio for the day."

Actually, he'd spent hours the night before thinking about what Lissa had said, and searching his heart. This morning, remembering the appointment for the bridal gown fitting that had been such a hot topic of discussion at the shower, he'd decided to drive to San Antonio to waylay Jenny.

At the last minute Todd had begged to come along, and Rob hadn't had the heart to refuse. He was glad now that he hadn't. The boy seemed to serve as a natural buffer, making both highly charged accusations and declarations of affection inappropriate.

Jenny was thinking the same thing. She smiled at Todd again, feeling more at ease than she'd felt in days. "Nice to meet you, Todd. I thought you looked a little familiar. You're the image of your mama."

Todd plainly couldn't decide whether he should be pleased or disgusted with her comment, but he did manage to give her a token thank-you. Then he turned to look at his uncle. "I'm hungry."

"It *is* lunchtime," Rob said agreeably. "And, look, there's the food court area right over there. Will you join us, Jenny?"

Jenny hesitated, longing to spend time with Rob, but knowing she shouldn't take the risk. Yet how personal could the conversation get with a child at the table?

Todd looked up at her and gave her another gap-toothed smile. "Please?"

Jenny's heart melted, and she gave in to the impulse. "Okay, if you really want me to."

Rob restrained his grin until Jenny turned and began to walk toward the table-filled mall courtyard and the assortment of fast-food restaurants that bordered it. Then he leaned over and whispered to Todd, "Good work, pardner."

He and his small accomplice exchanged conspiratorial winks and reached out to slap each other's palms.

Jenny cast a curious glance over her shoulder at the sound. All she saw were expressions that were entirely too innocent. She had the sneaking suspicion that Rob had planned this whole encounter. In her innermost self, she was glad. If she were very, very careful, she might be able to cheat fate. She might be able to steal one last hour with the man she loved.

"Remember the time you set off the ceiling sprinklers in Mr. Calvin's class?"

Rob was floating on the sound of Jenny's laughter. "I remember that it ruined that expensive new sweater you were wearing, and you wouldn't speak to me for a week."

"Well, it seems funny now!"

Rob stared at her face, wanting to memorize it, wanting to freeze this moment in time. All through lunch they had been reminiscing about the past, carefully avoiding all mention of the present and the future. He could have gone on that way all day, but time was fast running out and nothing had been resolved between them.

He looked down at Todd. The little boy was sitting by his side, soaking in their conversation while he finished up the last drops of his cherry cola. Trying to act nonchalant, as if they hadn't rehearsed it all down to the last detail, Rob pulled out a handful of quarters. "I bet you'd love to go to that video arcade over there, wouldn't you, Todd?"

For one heart-stopping second, he thought the boy was going to refuse. Then Todd jumped up from the table and took the quarters in both hands, carefully transferring them to his pockets. "I like video games," he said. "But I like candy bars even more."

Looking into the guileless green eyes, Rob recognized attempted blackmail when he saw it. "*If* you're good," he said, emphasizing the if, "I'll buy you a candy bar to take home. You can eat it after dinner."

Todd apparently decided to quit while he was ahead. "Don't forget," he called out as he headed for the video games.

"As if you'd let me," Rob muttered, hoping Maggie never heard about the sugar spree he'd taken her son on today.

He watched Todd go, congratulating himself on how well his strategy was working. He'd chosen the table because it was perfectly situated in relation to the video arcade. He could keep an eye on Todd, but the boy would be out of earshot.

He could see Jenny had taken note of that fact, too. A tension had seeped into her posture, a tension that hadn't been present before. She reached for her purse, and he knew he didn't have any time to lose.

Taking a deep breath, he plunged in. "Last night, Lissa confirmed something that I'd suspected all along—you planned on marrying me, not Keel."

Jenny's shoulders slumped and she sighed inwardly. For the past hour she'd been pretending. Pretending that nothing had changed between her and Rob. Pretending that the wedding on Saturday was going to be theirs. Imagining that someday they would be sharing a lunch at the mall with a little boy like Todd, a little boy all their own. All the time she'd known that the moment would come when she couldn't pretend any longer. Now that it was here, she didn't know if she could bear it.

She was so sick of fighting, so sick of lying. Wearily, she resigned herself to one more round. "Obviously, I didn't tell Lissa everything—a good thing seeing how she ran off at the mouth with you."

"She was trying to help."

"I'll just bet she was," Jenny snapped, feeling an unexpected resurgence of last night's jealousy. "And just how far did she go trying to help you, Rob? All the way to that big brass bed of hers?"

She moved to get up, but he put his hand over hers, holding her still with a touch. "Only as far as the dining room, Jen. I went to her house intending to start up with her again, but I didn't. I couldn't. All I could do was think about you."

Relief flooded through Jenny like a warm tide. "I— I don't know what to say."

"Then don't say anything. Just listen. I owe you an apology."

"An apology?" Jenny echoed, thinking she must have heard wrong.

"I spent a lot of time last night thinking about the things you've been saying, about how I held back and didn't really want to make a commitment. You were right. I wanted you, but not enough to give up everything else."

He looked into her eyes, willing her to understand. "If you had pushed, I would have chosen you. I would have given up my freedom. You didn't, so I let things ride. I guess I thought you'd always be there, waiting."

Jenny knew she ought to say something, ought to stop him before things went too far. But she needed to hear what he had to say more than she needed air to breathe.

"When I was finally ready for commitment, you weren't anymore—at least, not with me. I'm to blame for that. But I'm all grown up now, and I'm sorry I took you for granted. I didn't mean to. If you could find it in your heart to give me another chance, Jen, I promise not to make the same mistake. Not ever again."

Jenny's hand opened, then closed around his in a spasm of ecstasy and pain. It was all she'd ever dreamed of hearing him say. And it had come too late. Too late for her. Too late for them.

"I wish..." she began, her voice thick with unshed tears, "I wish that I could give you what you're asking for, Rob. I'd do almost anything, sacrifice almost anything to give that chance to you and to myself. But it's just not possible."

Somehow Rob had been sure that his lack of maturity had been the one real issue standing between them. Despite Jenny's denials, he'd been just as sure that she still cared. Had he been wrong? He felt a flash of near panic at the thought.

"Don't say that, Jenny. Anything's possible if you want it badly enough. All you have to do is say the word. I'll take care of Keel."

Jenny began to tremble, wanting to say that word but knowing she couldn't. Then help came from an unexpected quarter. Her fiancé's angry voice cut through the tense silence with all the grace of a carelessly wielded meat cleaver.

"I've been looking all over this damned mall for you, Jenny. What in the hell are you doing with Emory, and just what have you been telling him?"

"I ran into Rob by accident, and I haven't told him anything," Jenny protested.

"Good. Keep it that way. You made a deal with me, honey. You don't hold your end up, you live with the consequences."

Letting go of Jenny's hand, Rob got to his feet. "Now just what is that supposed to mean?"

Keel blew a cloud of cigar smoke into Rob's face. "Mind your own business, *Row-bare-toe.*"

Rob turned to Jenny, who was moving by him, moving toward Keel. "What is he talking about, Jen? Tell me!"

It would be so easy, so easy to tell him. And so hard to live with herself afterward. "Don't do this to me," she pleaded.

"Don't do this to us!"

Her heart breaking, she gave him the only answer she could. "There isn't any 'us' anymore."

"Damn it—"

"*Row-bare-toe*, sometimes I wonder if you understand English."

Rob felt his control give with an almost audible snap. He took a step forward and grabbed Keel by the collar. But before he had time to follow through, a big hand broke his grip and forced him back.

Travis loomed above him, looking as fearsome as judgment day and just as unavoidable. "Please, Mr. Emory, do us both a favor. Just sit down and let them leave."

It wasn't fear that kept Rob from retaliating. It was the genuine concern he saw in the bigger man's eyes. With a feeling of wonder, he realized that it would truly pain Travis to have to pound him into the concrete. Somehow that made him back down when no amount of threats would have. Still, he wasn't ready to give up. "Jenny..."

Shaking her head, Jenny backed away. This had gone too far already. Rob had almost gotten hurt, and it was all her fault for wavering, for failing to stand behind her decision. Well, from now on it would be different. "I'm marrying Jack in return for the security he can give me, Rob. That's the deal I made with him. By my own choice, of my own free will. I'm sorry if your ego won't let you accept that. I guess you haven't grown up that much, after all."

Rob watched the three of them walk away, aching, angry, and even more confused than he'd been before the encounter. Was he chasing phantoms, the victim of an inflated ego? Or was Jenny being coerced into marriage? And even if she was, how could he do anything about the situation if she refused to cooperate?

"Who were those two jerks?"

Rob felt a small, supportive hand slide into his, and looked down to see the defiant, frightened expression on Todd's face. "Nobody important," he said, trying to make light of the situation.

"But Jenny said she was going to marry the little one."

Rob smiled, pleased with Todd's description of Keel—although, to give the man his due, anyone would look small standing next to Travis. "Well, that's up to her."

"You like her, don't you?"

"Yeah, I do."

The boy patted Rob's back consolingly. "My mom and Jude used to argue like you and Jenny, but they really love each other now."

Rob sighed and gently pushed Todd in the direction of a chair. "Yeah, well sometimes there's a happy ending to a story and sometimes there isn't," he said, taking a seat himself.

"I like stories with happy endings a whole lot better than stories with sad ones," Todd informed his new uncle. Then he changed the subject with childlike abruptness. "When is my mom coming home? She calls me every day on the phone, but I still miss her anyway."

"You know she'll be back on Saturday. That's just five days from now." Five days until Jenny married Keel. He pushed the thought away with an effort. Todd was the one who needed comforting right now. He'd been so wrapped up in himself lately that he hadn't realized that the child really *was* missing his mother.

"Todd, your mama and Jude love you a lot, but right now they need just a little time by themselves so that they can get to know each other better. You can understand that, can't you?"

Todd gave him a look that was plainly mutinous. "I guess so."

With an inward sigh, Rob gave up. Todd looked as depressed as he felt. No matter what he said, the boy wouldn't feel any better until Maggie came home. However, there was a temporary remedy that would probably appeal to Todd as much as it appealed to him. Rob crossed his arms and leaned his elbows on the table. "What if we forget about that candy bar and buy some hot-fudge sundaes instead?"

Todd sat up straight in his chair. "With nuts and whipped cream and a cherry?"

"You bet."

As Rob started toward the ice-cream concession, he thought of the grin on Todd's face and wished he was still young enough to find forgetfulness so easily.

"Good night, flea bait."

Stifling a yawn, Rob gave Brandy's neck an affectionate pat and closed the stall door behind him. It had been one long, exhausting day.

This morning he'd had to scramble to finish the chores he'd set aside for himself before he could leave for San Antonio. Then he and Todd hadn't returned until late afternoon, and he'd had to play catch-up again. Now it was after dark, he'd missed dinner, and he was still no closer to resolving the situation with Jenny than he had been this morning.

He was halfway to the ranch manager's house where he and his mother lived when he noticed the light and laughter coming from the building that served as a combination mess hall and rec room for the hands.

His jaw tightening, he changed course. The water gap was still down, and he was in just the mood to enjoy confronting Will about it.

As he opened the screen door and stepped into the big room, he saw that a poker game was in progress. A couple of the married hands and all of the single ones were present. All except for Will.

He approached the table, looking at each face in turn. "Where's Will? I didn't see him around today."

Jesse Butler rearranged his cards and shrugged without looking up. That response was eloquent compared to the others in the room.

Taking a step closer to the table, Rob tried again. "What about you, Larry? Do you know where Will is?"

Larry Truman rubbed his chin and looked thoughtful. "I did hear that someone saw a Diamond cowboy out San Antonio way this mornin'."

Dave Applegate widened his eyes so far that they looked about to pop out of his head. When he spoke, his tone was just as comically exaggerated. "Now what do you suppose a Diamond hand would be doin' all the way over there?"

Larry looked directly at Rob. "I heard the man was chasin' a filly who'd already been roped."

Rob could hear the anticipation in the suddenly quiet room. They were waiting for his reaction with all the eagerness of school children straining to hear the last bell on a Friday afternoon. Despite his rising blood pressure, he refused to be the evening's entertainment.

"That sure does sound a lot like Will," he said blandly. "When he gets back, tell him I want to talk to him."

He had closed the door and stepped outside before the first hoot of laughter reached him. His ears burning, he walked the short distance to his mother's house, fuming all the way.

When he opened the door, the first person he saw was Todd. The child was sitting in the living room in front of the TV, munching on cookies.

"Haven't you had enough sweets today?"

Both Todd and Rob's mother, Nilda, looked up in obvious surprise at Rob's sharp tone.

"Do you feel like talking about it?" his mother asked with her usual perception.

Sighing, Rob hung his hat on the rack by the door. He was about to cover up with a light remark, when suddenly he knew that he wanted to tell her. He wanted to get it all off his chest before he lashed out at some other innocent bystander.

"I followed Jenny to San Antonio today and talked her into having lunch with me. The men just tried to give me a hard time about it. I'd really like to get my hands on the meddling fool who told them my business."

"I told them."

Rob looked down at Todd in surprise. The boy had come to stand beside him, his expression a study in remorse. "I'm sorry, Rob. I didn't know it was wrong to tell."

Pulling the child close for a hug, Rob felt the anger drain out of him, leaving a weariness that seemed to be bone-deep. "It's okay. It didn't amount to anything."

"You sure?"

"Yeah, I'm sure."

Rob patted the boy on the back and watched him return to the television. Then he sank onto one of the dining room chairs.

"I kept your dinner warm," his mother said, placing a steaming plate of food in front of him.

"Thanks, Mama. I'm sorry I came in so late." He began to eat automatically, hardly noticing what he put in his mouth.

Nilda brought a carafe of coffee and two cups to the table and seated herself across from him.

A heart-to-heart talk was in the air and Rob didn't know if he could deal with that right now. He met his mother's concerned gaze and tried to project an aura of confidence and composure. It wasn't easy.

Her olive skin flawless, her dark hair perfectly coiffed, Nilda Vasquez Emory, the head housekeeper for the Double Diamond, had the regal bearing of a queen. But she'd been only a maid on the Diamond when Jude's father, Ed Tanner, had won the ranch in a poker game.

Ed had already been engaged to another woman— not that that had stopped him from falling in love with Nilda and getting her pregnant. Tanner had gone on to marry his wealthy fiancée, and had arranged for his ranch manager, Ben Emory, to marry Nilda. Ben had been the only father Jude had known or wanted to know until Ed's secretary, Margret Brolin, had come to the ranch for Tanner's funeral, bringing her employer's taped autobiography with her.

Nilda was a wealthy woman now. Tanner's will had left the ranch manager's house where she'd always lived to her, as well as the rights to all of his popular mystery novels. She had resigned her job as housekeeper and had only postponed her own extensive travel plans so that she could baby-sit for Todd while Jude and Margret were on their honeymoon.

"Roberto, why don't you go to bed? You seem so tired."

Focusing on his mother's face, Rob realized that he had almost nodded off at the dinner table. "I thought you wanted to talk to me."

Nilda put down her coffee cup and reached out to touch his hand. "I am here in case *you* want to talk."

For a moment Rob wished he were a child again, that his mother could apply a bandage, kiss the hurt, and make everything better. But he wasn't a child and there was nothing she could do. He was about to tell her so, when he stopped and forced his weary brain to think about it. Maybe there was something, after all.

"Mama, who would you ask if you wanted to find out why Jenny is marrying Jack Keel? She won't tell me the real reason, and I can't get close enough to Keel to force the answer out of him."

Nilda sipped her coffee and thought for a moment. "I would ask Tate. He loves Jenny more than anything else on earth, and she feels the same way about him. If she confided in anyone, it would be her father."

"I already thought of that. But when I went to Jenny's house the other night, I got the impression Tate was definitely on my side—and as much in the dark as I am. If he had known anything that would help me stop the marriage, he would've told me then."

He covered his mouth to stifle a persistent yawn. "It doesn't really matter, anyway, I guess. After what happened today, I'd have to be a fool to keep chasing Jenny."

"Do you love her?"

Rob hesitated, struggling between truth and pride.

Nilda smiled at his reaction. "If you do love her—
really love her—don't let pride or what anyone else
says stop you from going after her. Even if she rejects
you in the end, you will have tried your hardest to get
what you want. There is never any shame in that."

She picked up her cup and saucer and got to her
feet.

Rob stood, skirted the table, and put his arms
around her. "You can still make it all better, can't you,
Mama?"

Nilda looked up at her son inquiringly. "What on
earth are you talking about?"

"Nothing important." He gave her a kiss on the
forehead and turned in the direction of his bedroom.
For once he felt that he could fall asleep as soon as his
head was on the pillow—or maybe before. He was
struggling to keep his eyes open even now.

"Roberto?"

Reluctantly, he turned back to look at his mother.

She pressed her lips together, showing an uncer-
tainty that he'd rarely seen her display. "There are
many reasons a woman might feel that she has to
marry a man," she said finally. "Be sure that you
consider all of them."

Then she turned and walked into the kitchen, leaving him standing there alone and more than a little
confused. His mother was sometimes frank, often
profound. But she could also be so careful not to tread
on another's feelings that she ended up being down-
right vague. Right now, he was too tired to even try to
puzzle out the real meaning of her words.

Tomorrow. Tomorrow, he'd ask his mother what
she'd been trying to tell him. Tomorrow, he'd con-

front Will. And maybe he'd even go have a talk with Tate—just to cover all the bases.

He was suddenly very sure that he wasn't ready to give up on Jenny. Not just yet.

Chapter Five

"Will, damn you, I know you're in there!" Rob jerked open the door of the trailer and walked inside.

A shaft of early morning sunlight hit the huddled figure on the bed full in the face. "For the love of God!" Will groaned.

He twisted around, pulling the sheet up to cover his eyes.

Rob stepped over a pile of dirty laundry and approached the small bed. Ruthlessly, he grabbed the sheet and jerked it back down.

Will squinted up at his tormentor, his face contorted with pain. "Damn, Rob!" he said, his voice only a little above a whisper. "Can't you see I'm sick?"

"Sick?" Rob laughed out loud, and Will clutched his head in reaction. "I'd be sick, too, if I'd just been out on a two-day drunk. That's a new record, even for you!"

Somehow Will managed a weak-looking smile. "Well, I wasn't drinking all the time. That little blond waitress finally said yes."

"I don't care if you scored with ten of her friends and left a trail of empty tequila bottles from here to El Paso! You have a job to do, Will. Just because my brother's out of town doesn't mean you're on vacation."

Will made an effort to sit up, then fell back with a moan. "Just give me a couple of hours."

Rob shook his head decisively. "I gave you a whole day. That water gap is *still* down."

"Can't you take care of it?"

Rob squeezed his eyes shut for a moment, trying hard to resist the call to violence. "Why in the hell should I do that?"

"'Cause you're my friend. I sure covered for you enough times—before you got so high and mighty."

Looking down at Will's green-tinged skin, Rob bit back a detailed description of what the man could do with himself. What Will said was true enough, and it hadn't been that long ago. But, all at once, it seemed to Rob that all that had happened years ago, in some other lifetime. He resented being held accountable for it now.

"All right, Will. I'll do it, but it's the last time. You hear me? After this, we're even."

Without waiting for a reply, he stalked out of the trailer, sending two empty beer cans bouncing down the trailer steps ahead of him.

He slammed the door behind him, and actually enjoyed the agonized groan of protest that resulted.

The next several minutes were spent loading old fence posts and wire, staples, and the various tools

Rob needed on the bed of his pickup. Then he went
inside the house to change into an old T-shirt, shorts,
tennis shoes and a baseball cap.

As he got behind the wheel of the truck, his
thoughts were still occupied by a brooding anger directed at Will. But as he started toward the creek that
separated the Landon place from the Diamond, his
thoughts turned inevitably toward Jenny.

Despite his tiredness, their confrontation in the mall
yesterday had caused him to lose a lot of sleep. He still
couldn't figure out what the hell was going on between her and Keel. He wouldn't have minded taking
the other man apart piece by piece until Keel decided
to tell him. But with Travis standing guard, he'd never
get close enough. That left Tate and Jenny.

Jenny, for whatever reason, wasn't talking. Tate, he
could try to touch base with later today—assuming he
could catch the man alone. The way Jenny watched
over her father, that was assuming a lot.

As he approached the creek, his thoughts refocused
on the task at hand. Then he blinked, wondering if he
were imagining things or if what he saw was real.
Jenny was standing knee-deep in the water, using wire
pliers to pull an old staple out of the one post that the
flood waters from the recent rain had left standing.

She looked up at the sound of his truck. He was still
too far away to read her expression, but he could
imagine the story it would tell: apprehension, uncer-
tainty. She would be expecting him to be furious after
what she'd said yesterday. In fact, she'd be counting
on using his anger against him. Using it to serve as a
barrier between them—a barrier that she could hide
behind. But she was in for a surprise. He'd come to the
conclusion that no amount of pushing from him was

going to make her confide in him. Instead, it was making her pull further away.

From now on, things were going to be different. If she wouldn't open herself up, then he would talk to her about his feelings. He would speak to her emotions, to her memories, and hope that she responded. Was it worth the effort and the risk? The old Rob wouldn't have thought so. The new Rob had just begun to fight.

He stopped the truck near the water's edge, across the fence from where her Jeep was parked. He killed the engine and swung out, letting his gaze roam over her. Whatever resentment he might have been harboring dissolved in a fierce rush of desire. Either there was something innately erotic about a woman wearing a one-piece black bathing suit, work gloves, and a straw cowboy hat, or he still had a serious case of the hots for Jenny Landon.

"Mornin', Jenny. What are you doing out here?"

Jenny felt his gaze burn into her like a hot branding iron. She fumbled with the pliers and narrowly escaped giving herself a nasty bruise.

How could she answer his question? She couldn't tell him that she was strung out tighter than any wire, wanting to confide in him, wanting the comfort only he could give her. She couldn't tell him that she wasn't able to force down enough food to keep a bird alive. That she was sleeping less and less as each night went by, tortured by the knowledge that with every hour that passed, she drew an hour closer to losing him forever.

Finally she'd had to do something to get her mind off the approaching wedding or go stark raving mad. She'd jumped into her Jeep and gone tearing around the ranch like a race-car driver with a death wish.

That's when she'd noticed the washed-out water gap. Almost humming with satisfaction, she'd gone back to the house to change and get the supplies she needed. It had seemed like a heaven-sent opportunity to work herself into exhaustion—until Rob had shown up.

Now she squirmed under his regard, too aware that her own repressed desires were dangerously close to bursting into flame. Her mind desperately searched for a plausible excuse for her presence. At last, she hit upon one that was ideal because it was the truth.

She shrugged with all the nonchalance she could muster. "If I left it like this, Daddy would see it and try to fix it himself. He still gets out on old Tillie every day. And he still thinks he's a rancher—even if we did sell off all the cattle after his first heart attack."

Rob had nearly forgotten that Jenny's father was a very sick man. Tate had always seemed so strong, so full of life, that it was hard to think of him as a semi-invalid. Still, Rob recalled, the Landons had always been able to live comfortably. There were a couple of oil wells on the property that were still pumping crude, and Tate had built up a nice little business selling the fine, custom-made saddles he turned out in his workshop.

His tennis shoes sinking a good two inches into the muddy bottom, Rob walked down into the creek. He didn't come to a stop until he was a foot away from Jenny. Until he was close enough to see the apprehension in those smoke-gray eyes. Close enough to count the tiny beads of perspiration above her upper lip. Aroused enough to wish he could lick them away one by one.

Instead he reached out and took the pliers from her. "Tate knows that the Diamond has always kept up this gap. Not that we don't appreciate a little help from our neighbors now and then.''

Jenny recognized an invitation when she heard one. The smart thing would be for her to hightail it out of here and leave the damned fence to him. But she hadn't been acting very smart lately. Even if she couldn't touch him, she wanted to stay close to him, to hear his voice. The longing to stay was a physical ache.

She hesitated for a second too long. He pulled the last staple, and she stooped to retrieve the broken wire it had been holding.

They worked together for the rest of the morning, planting posts, stretching wire, and stapling it into place.

Rebuilding a water gap was a hard job, and, normally, Jenny would have considered it a thankless one because it would have to be done all over again after the next heavy rain. The fence across the creek was temporary, designed to wash away under the pressure of water-driven debris. If it had been built more securely, it would have dragged the permanent fences on both creek banks down with it when it finally gave way. But today, none of that mattered to Jenny. She was grateful for any chance to work off the physical and emotional frustration that had been building up inside her for far too long.

She was holding the final strand of wire, waiting for Rob to drive the staple, when he let his arm drop back to his side.

''I just thought of something, Jen.''

She looked up and saw that he was smiling at her again. ''What?'' she asked, a trifle breathlessly.

She was flustered and confused by his continuing good mood. After what had happened in the mall yesterday, he should have been madder than blazes at her. Instead he was the old Rob she had always known and loved, the naturally considerate charmer who could melt the heart of any woman—and *had* with maddening regularity. There was nothing to fight against, no anger she could use to keep him at a distance. She didn't know how much longer she could bear it.

He was talking again, megawatt smile damped down, eyes scanning the horizon. "If I put these staples in, the fence will be finished. You'll be on that side, and I'll be on this side. That's going to make it awfully hard for us to have lunch together."

"L-lunch?" A part of Jenny stood by objectively observing the blushing and the stammering, and recognized herself for the fool she was. Look at all the trouble sharing a simple lunch had caused yesterday! Was she going to participate in a repeat performance? He might be all smiles now, but sooner or later, the other shoe would fall.

The sensible part of her knew all that. But it wasn't that part that reached out and grasped the hand Rob held out to her. Carefully, she stepped over the strands of barbed wire they'd already strung.

Suddenly she was standing so close to him that their bodies were almost touching. Jenny looked up and found herself getting lost in his eyes—eyes too beautiful to be wasted on a man. Like a coin thrown into a wishing well, she sank into their dark, bottomless depths without leaving a ripple.

Rob was on the edge of giving in to desire. He'd been watching her all morning. Watching the water droplets run down her taut thighs, watching her bathing suit ride up to reveal the firm lines of her bottom, following the beads of sweat as they slid down into the shadow between the soft curves of her breasts. He wanted to take her into his arms and kiss her until they both forgot that anyone or anything else existed. But more than that, he wanted Jenny to stay with him after the kiss was over. He wanted forever.

With an inward sigh, Rob released her hand, turned away, and walked toward his truck.

Jenny was surprised and unsettled by his desertion. She could have sworn he'd been about to kiss her. She should have felt relieved. Instead she felt bereft.

Trying to give himself a chance to regain some control over his feelings, Rob took his time retrieving a bag of food from the passenger seat, and an old blanket from the truck bed. Although food had been the last thing on his mind this morning, he was glad that his mother had foisted a big lunch on him. Not only because the work had restored his flagging appetite, but because eating lunch gave him an excuse to spend more time with Jenny.

He slipped out of his wet tennis shoes, leaving them to dry in the sun. Then he cleared a space in the shade of a pecan tree and spread the blanket. Stretching out on his side, he patted the empty space next to him.

Eyeing him warily, Jenny left her shoes beside his. She knelt down on the far side of the blanket and took off her hat. Seizing the bag of food, she pulled it around in front of her.

Rob watched in growing amusement as she took sandwiches, fruit and cookies from the bag and lined all the food up between them. "Well, Jen, you can say you built a fence *and* a wall today."

Jenny looked up at him with a frown, then realized what he meant. The glint of mischief in his eyes dared her, and she found herself responding recklessly. "They're both only temporary."

Suddenly overwhelmingly hungry, she grabbed a sandwich, unwrapped it, and took a big bite.

For a moment Rob watched her speculatively. Then he, too, started eating, determined to satisfy at least one hunger.

Sharing sweet, hot coffee from a single thermos cup, they ate in companionable silence. Both were ravenous and both felt strangely at peace in each other's company—as if a truce had finally been called after a long and bloody battle. It was easy to think only of the moment because now was all they had.

Jenny was the first to call it quits. Holding her stomach, she fell back onto the blanket with a soft moan of defeat. "And I was afraid there wouldn't be enough for two. I should have remembered your mama's lunches."

"I thought you said you were hungry?"

"I never could keep up with you."

Rob finished the last of the cookies and set the remains of the meal aside. Moving as close to Jenny as he dared, he lay back and joined her in contemplating the clouds through the leafy green canopy above them.

He was quiet for several minutes, wanting to broach the subject of Keel, but knowing how the confrontation would end. Instead he racked his brain for some neutral comment. Something nonthreatening—and maybe even a little romantic.

"The sky's so blue it almost hurts your eyes," he said with uncharacteristic nervousness. He turned to

PLAY

SILHOUETTE'S

LUCKY HEARTS GAME

AND GET

- ★ FREE BOOKS
- ★ A FREE CRYSTAL PENDANT NECKLACE
- ★ AND MUCH MORE

TURN THE PAGE AND
DEAL YOURSELF IN →

PLAY "LUCKY HEARTS" AND GET ...

★ Exciting Silhouette Romance™ novels — FREE

★ Plus a Crystal Pendant Necklace — FREE

THEN CONTINUE YOUR LUCKY STREAK WITH A SWEETHEART OF A DEAL

1. Play Lucky Hearts as instructed on the opposite page.

2. Send back this card and you'll receive brand-new Silhouette Romance™ novels. These books have a cover price of $2.75 each, but they are yours to keep absolutely free.

3. There's no catch. You're under no obligation to buy anything. We charge nothing — ZERO — for your first shipment. And you don't have to make any minimum number of purchases — not even one!

4. The fact is thousands of readers enjoy receiving books by mail from the Silhouette Reader Service. They like the convenience of home delivery...they like getting the best new novels months before they're available in bookstores...and they love our discount prices!

5. We hope that after receiving your free books you'll want to remain a subscriber. But the choice is yours — to continue or cancel, anytime at all! So why not take us up on our invitation, with no risk of any kind. You'll be glad you did!

You'll look like a million dollars when you wear this lovely necklace! Its cobra-link chain is a generous 18" long, and the multi-faceted Austrian crystal sparkles like a diamond!

SILHOUETTE'S

With a coin — scratch off the silver card and check below to see how many gifts you get.

YES! I have scratched off the silver card. Please send me all the free gifts for which I qualify. I understand that I am under no obligation to purchase any books, as explained on the back and on the opposite page.

215 CIS AND5
(U-SIL-R-02/94)

NAME

ADDRESS _____ APT.

CITY _____ STATE _____ ZIP

Twenty-one gets you 4 free books, and a free crystal pendant necklace

Twenty gets you 4 free books

Nineteen gets you 3 free books

Eighteen gets you 2 free books

THE SILHOUETTE READER SERVICE™: HERE'S HOW IT WORKS

Accepting free books places you under no obligation to buy anything. You may keep the books and gift and return the shipping statement marked "cancel". If you do not cancel, about a month later we'll send you 6 additional novels, and bill you just $2.19 each plus 25¢ delivery and applicable sales tax, if any.* That's the complete price—and compared to cover prices of $2.75 each—quite a bargain! You may cancel at anytime, but if you choose to continue, every month we'll send you 6 more books, which you may either purchase at the discount price ... or return at our expense and cancel your subscription.

*Terms and prices subject to change without notice. Sales tax applicable in N.Y.

Jenny to gauge her reaction and realized with a shock that while he'd been waxing poetic, she'd fallen asleep.

He gazed at her for a long time, reveling in the knowledge that he could finally look his fill. Ever so gently, he stroked the stray tendrils of hair that had escaped her braid. He studied the shifting patterns of shadow and light that played across her face with each whim of the breeze. He watched her lashes quiver against her cheek and listened to the deep sigh of her breathing. And for the first time in his life, he knew the true meaning of temptation.

He was aching, bowstring-taut with wanting her. If he came to her now, he knew that he could slip in under her defenses. She would be his at last. But, moral considerations aside, would she ever forgive him? He knew the answer to that as well as he knew his own name. He would lose more than he could ever hope to win.

With a sigh, he resigned himself to stealing only what he knew she wouldn't begrudge him. Easing closer, he put one arm around her waist and laid his head on one soft shoulder.

Being that near her should have made him even more uncomfortable. Instead his body began to relax, and his eyelids grew heavy. He frowned, wondering at his reaction. True, he hadn't been sleeping much at night, and he had worked hard this morning. But there was something else.

Then he realized what it was. Now, holding Jenny in his arms, was the first time he'd felt any sense of ease or contentment since the day she'd called to break off with him. He was no closer to solving the enigma of Jenny's defection than he had been that day, but, all at once, that didn't seem important. Only this moment was important. And, for this moment, he held everything he wanted in his arms.

A smile on his face, Rob drifted into the sweetest sleep he'd ever known.

Jenny opened her eyes feeling a vague sense of emptiness and loss. Squinting at the sunlit sky above her, she tried to pinpoint what was bothering her. She remembered having lunch and closing her eyes to rest for a moment. But now something wasn't right. For a second, she couldn't put her finger on it. Then she realized that it was the position of the sun. It had to be late afternoon, which meant she'd been asleep for hours!

Shooting to a sitting position, she looked around her and felt an almost physical sense of relief when she saw Rob standing by the creek. As she watched, he slipped his T-shirt off over his head and bent to submerge the garment in the water. Then he pulled it free, the muscles in his arms rippling as he wrung it out.

Her throat suddenly dry, Jenny watched him run the shirt over his face, then down across his chest and belly. His skin a natural golden tan, he looked like a young Indian warrior performing a purification ceremony—or some movie actor in a sensual scene from the latest blockbuster.

But she knew he was only an everyday working man—the man she wanted to come home to at the end of every day and go to bed with every night. It had seemed a possible dream until Jack had come to see her at school a few weeks ago.

Rob turned and caught her watching, and she swallowed the sudden ache in her throat and forced a smile. He gave her a grin that was teasing and wicked all at once. "Hey, sleepyhead!"

"Hey, yourself."

He spread the wet shirt out on the hood of his truck to dry, and came over to flop down on the blanket again. Jenny eyed the water droplets glistening on his chest and hair, and had to restrain herself from touching him. Instead she looked away, out across the fence to her father's land.

"Were you watching me sleep all this time?" she asked, a little self-consciously.

"Nope. I just woke up a minute ago myself." He regarded her steadily. "I did hold you in my arms while you slept. Just like I did the night of the senior prom. Remember?"

Jenny couldn't help smiling. "How could I forget? We were parked at Lookout Hill, waiting for the sunrise, and we both fell asleep."

"And when we woke up, I kissed you for the first time."

Jenny avoided his gaze, knowing hers would reveal too much. "It was the first time any boy had kissed me," she confessed.

Rob raised an eyebrow in surprise. "You never told me that."

She picked a twig up off the blanket and threw it back into the grass with more force than necessary. "Honestly, Rob! I was a shy, clumsy, plain little bookworm who'd never been out on a date before. Who did you think had been kissing me?"

Rob sat up and leaned closer to her, intrigued by the information she was giving him. "I didn't think about it at all, I guess. And you weren't ever clumsy or plain. You were always pretty."

"Oh, please. Spare me!" Jenny crossed her arms over her chest and looked down at her lap, all her old feelings of inferiority coming back with astonishing clarity.

Rob frowned, puzzled by her reaction. "You *were* pretty."

"I didn't even have a date for the prom. You only asked me because you felt sorry for me."

Wishing she'd look at him, he leaned even closer. "I didn't feel sorry for you. You wanted to go. You didn't have a date, and I was your friend."

"That amounts to the same thing," she said cynically, still feeling the hurt. "Of course, there was an advantage for you, too. It was easier to take me than to chose one of your girlfriends and risk offending the others."

Rob couldn't believe she'd been nursing that imagined hurt all these years. Thinking back, he examined his motives honestly, and shook his head. "I guess that's true. But that's not why I asked you."

Feeling a surge of warmth she couldn't deny, Jenny looked up and searched his eyes. "Really?"

"Really."

"Then it was sweet of you. It's a night I'll remember all my life. It was the first time I felt attractive. The first time I felt like a woman."

"I'll always remember it, too."

Jenny smiled, disbelieving. "I'll bet you don't even remember the color of the dress I was wearing."

Slowly, Rob opened his hand to reveal the small, lavender blossom he'd picked a few moments before. "Your dress was the color of this flower. I was thinking of that when I picked it."

Jenny reached out and took the tiny flower, no words able to pass the emotion swelling in her throat.

"Jenny, I'm not lying when I say I remember that night. That's the night I first knew I wanted you."

Jenny shook her head vigorously, unwilling to believe. "No, that's not the way it was. I went away to college and you didn't ask me out on a date again until I came home for the summer two years later. By then, I had dated other men. My roommate had taught me about makeup and clothes. That's when you began to notice me."

Smiling at her interpretation, Rob gently corrected her. "I noticed you in a big way the night of the prom. It scared me so bad that I had to pull back for two whole years. It took that long before I decided I wanted you more than I was afraid of the things you made me feel."

He hesitated, wanting to go on, but unsure that his instincts were correct. He didn't know how Jenny would react. He only knew that, despite everything, he believed she cared for him. For some reason she wouldn't—or couldn't—open her heart to him. He had to be the one to take the chance if he ever hoped to find the key.

"I was scared because I was only eighteen years old, and I had already started to fall in love with you. I tried to hide from it, but I couldn't. I loved that girl, Jenny, but I love the woman even more."

He sat there, his heart in his eyes, and waited for her to break it.

But, at the moment, that was the furthest thought from Jenny's mind. The answering pledge trembled on her lips. She couldn't say the words, but she could show him how she felt. She couldn't marry him, but she could give him something that had always belonged to him. Something that Jack Keel had no right to.

Jenny slowly reached out and touched Rob's face, tracing the line of his cheek with unsteady fingers.

Rob sat perfectly still, hardly daring to breathe. Afraid that anything he did or said would break the spell he'd woven and negate the magic of Jenny's response.

Her lips touched his softly, tentatively, and the sweetness of it nearly brought tears to his eyes. "Oh, Jenny," he whispered. "I've missed you so much."

He returned her kiss with the same hesitancy, the same yearning. He leaned closer, his hand slipping beneath her hair to warm her neck, his thumb stroking the velvet line of her jaw.

Her tongue touched his lips lightly, asking permission to enter. He gave it willingly, opening his mouth, welcoming her inside.

Passion flared in spontaneous combustion, and they were both consumed by the flame. Jenny's hands swept up over the muscles on his arms, tracing every ridge and contour, then down over the smooth expanse of his chest.

Rob's arms tightened around her reflexively, and he took her down to the blanket. His mouth moved over hers as his fingers hooked under the straps of the bathing suit—the bathing suit that had been tormenting him for hours. Then he peeled the straps down her arms and away, baring her to the waist.

Moving beneath him, Jenny strained upward as his lips swept down over chin, neck and collarbone to the hard peak of one breast. He let his tongue trace it once and felt her responsive shiver echo in his own body.

Then he took it into his mouth and she moaned softly. When his fingers found the tip of her other breast, she called his name aloud.

Melting inside, Jenny felt her muscles contracting with every tug of his mouth. It was she who inched her suit down over her hips and kicked it away.

His fingers moved lower, touching her where she had never allowed him to touch her before. It hadn't been lack of wanting that had held her back—it had been fear. Fear that if she let him go that far, she wouldn't want to stop him from taking her completely. As the first shiver of pleasure washed through her, she knew that she'd been right.

But now she wanted him to take her. She wanted to give him a part of herself that would never belong to any other man. His mouth at her breast, his caressing fingers took away the last of her inhibitions. Her hand dropped down to fumble with the zipper of his pants.

Rob shivered at her hesitant touch, then covered her hand with his and showed her how. But instead of caressing him, she drew him toward her.

His thoughts whirling in incoherent patterns, his heart exulting, his body yearning, he positioned himself above her. It would take only a single thrust to complete his possession of her and only a few words from her to make the act meaningful.

"Say you love me, Jenny."

His voice penetrated the haze of passion surrounding her and tore at her heart. They were simple words and easy to say. But if she said them now, he would expect her to stand behind them. And that was something she wasn't free to do.

Tears in her eyes, she slowly shook her head.

Rob felt as if he'd suddenly been encased in ice. The passion drained out of him to be replaced by a raging mixture of anger and despair. His body still wanted her, but his heart couldn't stand the pain of having her, only to give her up again.

"I won't," he rasped, every word an effort. "I won't take you if I can't keep you!"

Quickly, before he could change his mind, he rolled away from her and straightened his clothes. Then with one anguished glance at her unclothed body, he got to his feet and jogged to his truck.

The engine roared to life and he tore away, leaving a long set of tire marks behind in the grass. The wet T-shirt he'd laid on the hood blew free and settled on the ground in a dirty white tangle.

Jenny felt a sob escape her throat. Just once she had wanted to share herself with him, to know the joy of the culmination of love. Just an hour with Rob before she had to go with Jack for a lifetime. But he hadn't allowed her even that much.

Shaking with pent-up emotion, she drew the blanket around her and let the tears come. They were the only comfort she had left.

Chapter Six

Rob watched the first pale light of dawn creep around the edge of the bedroom shade. Jenny was getting married in three days, and he was no closer to changing that fact than he had been the night of Jude's wedding.

Thinking over the events of the day before, he wondered at his own actions. Had he really refused to take Jenny, to take what he'd been wanting all these years?

Two weeks ago—two *days* ago—there might have been a far different outcome to that scene by the creek. If anyone had predicted then that Jenny would offer herself to him and that *he'd* be the one to walk away, he'd have laughed out loud. Even now he would rather have walked through a blizzard buck naked than try to explain his actions to another man. He was having a hard enough time coming to terms with them himself.

The decision to walk away had come from deep inside him, from a place he hadn't even dreamed existed. That part of him had wanted more than just a temporary possession of Jenny's body. He hadn't been willing to settle for only a physical release, and he still wasn't.

Confused and bone-tired, he dragged himself out of bed. He hardly recognized the man who looked back at him from the bathroom mirror. He was acting on instinct alone, with no precedent to guide him, no rule book to point the way. And so far he had gotten nowhere. He'd admitted that he loved her. That hadn't worked. What else could he do or say to change her mind?

The shrill ring of the phone pulled him away from the bathroom and his brooding thoughts. Throwing himself back onto the bed, he reached out an arm to snag the receiver. "Hello?"

"Hey, little brother! Are you feeling as good as I am right now?"

The question should have inspired tears, but Rob couldn't help smiling at the sheer happiness in his brother's voice. "Somehow, I tend to doubt that's possible. How's Acapulco?"

"I don't know. But this hotel room's great."

Rob chuckled at the old joke and, in the background, he heard the faint echo of feminine laughter come over the phone line. "Glad to hear you're enjoying yourself. Say hi to Maggie for me."

There was a woman's squeal and a few highly suggestive rustling sounds. Then Jude's voice came back on the line. "Maggie says hello. Listen, I just called to remind you to send someone to the airport for us on

Saturday morning. Otherwise, I just might be tempted to stay gone another week.''

At the mention of Saturday, Rob's smile vanished. He tried to think of words to fill the ensuing silence, but none came to mind. Jude's voice came over the wire, the tone subdued. ''The wedding's still on, then?''

''Yeah.'' It was an admission of defeat.

''You sure there's nothing I can do, *hermano?*''

Rob was about to refuse, when he suddenly realized there *was* something. He hadn't really given any serious thought to the future before, but now things were different. *He* was different. ''Jude...oh, hell, I don't even know how to say this.''

''Say it any way you want.''

''You know how you used to talk about how it would be when you inherited the Diamond?''

''And how a share of it would be yours? I haven't forgotten. Maggie and I were going to sit down with you and have a talk about it when we got back.''

Rob exhaled the breath he'd been holding, then took another as he realized that the hardest part lay ahead. ''I just need some land, Jude. Land that I can sell if I have to.''

There was a pause, a few seconds of silence that strung Rob's nerves out tight. ''I'd hate to think of some developer building a resort in my backyard, Rob. The damned dude ranch guests are bad enough.''

Rob twisted the phone cord around his hand until it threatened to cut off his circulation. ''It's not what I want, either. But it might come to that.''

''Well, that's up to you, *hermano.* Once the land's yours, you can do what you want with it. Maggie and

I figured a two-way split would be fair, land and profits. Half for us, half for you."

The phone cord snapped free as Rob sat up on the bed. "I . . . damn, Jude! I don't know what to say to that. I have no real right to any of it. Ed Tanner was your father, not mine."

"But your father was the one who worked the Diamond, who made it what it is today. Him, and us after him. Ben Emory was the only father I ever knew or wanted to know. And you're my only brother."

Rob was warmed by an affection that was more important than shared genes or material possessions could ever be. "You're sure?"

"I'm sure. I know you're worth it. I just hope Jenny is."

The certainty came from somewhere Rob couldn't name. "She is."

"Good. Tell Todd we'll call him at lunchtime. And you remember to send someone to the airport for us, little brother—or, I guarantee you, I'm gonna have some serious second thoughts."

There was another high-pitched squeal, and the line went dead in Rob's hands.

He looked at the receiver with a kind of dull shock. Jude, the man whose faithless first wife had left him with an abiding distrust of women, hadn't even rebuked him for being foolish enough to put his trust in a woman who was scheduled to marry another man. Instead, he'd understood. Rob knew that Maggie was responsible for Jude's newfound belief in love, and now, more than ever, he thanked God that she had come into his brother's life.

He thought about his own faith in Jenny, and he realized that his feelings for her ran even deeper than he'd dared imagine. For her, he was willing to risk two things he held sacred—the land and his brother's trust. The very idea of it was almost too scary for him to contemplate. And even more frightening was the possibility that he was taking the risk for nothing. He promised himself that before the day was over, the question would be settled—one way or the other.

Rob returned to the bathroom and started preparing for the day, bits of the conversation he'd had with his brother running through his mind. The most surprising thing of all was that Jude hadn't once asked about how things were going with his horses or with the men. For a man who usually spent twenty hours a day worrying about the Diamond and the other four dreaming about it, that was a miracle. Jude obviously had other priorities now. And he obviously trusted Rob to handle things on the ranch.

Rob finished buttoning his shirt and reached for his Stetson. He had never let his brother down before, and he sure as hell didn't intend to start now.

"Goin' huntin', Rob?"

Rob stepped into the stirrup and swung aboard the mare. Looking over at the group of hands gathered at the main corral, he waited for the old feeling of discomfort to appear. The feeling that warned him to cover up, to safeguard his pride. But nothing happened. It simply didn't matter anymore what the other men thought about him and Jenny. The only opinion he cared about was his own. He wondered at the change in his thinking, and reveled in the feeling of freedom that came with it.

"I guess you could call it hunting," he said easily. "I know what I want, and I'm going after it."

Will climbed down off the fence and came to stand close beside the mare. He spoke in a low voice, his tone more serious than Rob had ever heard it before.

"Listen, Rob. I'm your friend, and I gotta tell you. You're making a laughingstock of yourself over that woman."

A small smile appeared on Rob's lips. "What's a friend to you, Will?" he asked softly. "Someone to drink with and chase women with? Someone to help you pretend that time isn't passing and you aren't getting any older? Well, I'm all grown up now. You'll have to find someone else to play with."

He raised his voice until it carried clearly to the men at the corral. "From now on, I'm giving the orders on the Diamond. Anyone who has an objection to that can step on over here. I'll get down and we can settle the matter, man to man, once and for all. Otherwise, it's time to get to work."

The men exchanged startled, uneasy glances, but none appeared overeager to take him up on his offer. One by one, they slid down from the fence and went to their waiting horses. Rob looked down at Will, who was gazing up at him with a dull expression of surprise. "You, too, Will. Get a move on."

Will opened his mouth to object, then apparently thought better of it. Giving Rob one last assessing glance, he walked to his own mount and climbed into the saddle.

Rob waited until they had all ridden away, then he turned his mare toward the Landon ranch. He might have won one battle, but he knew it had been nothing compared to the one that lay ahead.

"Tate?" Rob walked through the open doorway and into the shed, blinking at the sudden change. At

first the interior seemed dark compared to the bright
sunlight outside, but once his eyes adjusted, Rob saw
that it was well-lit and spacious.

Tate was seated behind a worktable, incising an in-
tricate decorative pattern into a piece of leather. He
looked up as Rob approached and laid aside the tool
he'd been using.

"Don't stop on my account," Rob told him. "I always enjoy watching the master craftsman at work."

Tate smiled and waved him to a straight-back chair.
"Sorry to disappoint you, boy, but I need to rest my
eyes for a spell. At least now I have something to oc-
cupy me while I'm doin' it."

Rob sat in the proffered chair, leaned back, and
propped his ankle up on his knee. "I went up to the
house first, but no one answered the door."

"You try the windows?"

Rob felt the blood rush to his face at the veiled ref-
erence to his nocturnal visits to Jenny's bedroom. He
tried to think of some appropriate response. None
came to mind.

Chuckling, Tate slapped him on the knee. "That's
all right, boy. I'm only funnin' you. Jenny ain't here.
She went in to Layton City to do something for that
damned wedding."

Rob was both disappointed and encouraged. He'd
never have a better opportunity to talk to Tate. He
cleared his throat. "I guess you know how I feel about
Jenny, sir. So you can imagine how I feel about her
and Keel. She acts like she doesn't like him all that
much herself, but she won't back down from marrying him. And the only real reason she'll give me for

going through with it, is that she wants his money. Knowing Jenny, that answer makes no sense at all."

Tate nodded in agreement as he drew a tobacco pouch, some rolling papers and a book of matches out of a vest pocket. "It's enough to drive a man to drink."

"So there's nothing more to it? Nothing she's told you that I don't know?"

"If she had, son, I'd've been on the phone to you in a New York minute. But it's just as big a mystery to me as it is to you."

Rob hesitated, reluctant to offend or upset the older man. He'd been raised by the rule that you didn't mention another man's finances unless he broached the subject first—and then you let him do most of the talking. Only his feelings for Jenny made him push ahead.

"I've been thinking about what all she might need a lot of money for, and there's only one thing I've been able to come up with." He paused, trying to find a tactful way to phrase it. "I know...that is, you haven't been in the best of health and, well..."

"Don't tap dance around so much, boy," Tate admonished. "You're making me nervous." He finished rolling the homemade cigarette and licked the paper to seal it. "You know my heart's in bad shape and you want to know if I need the money for a transplant or some other medical nonsense."

Rob leaned forward in the chair, relieved by the other man's reaction. "Yes, sir, that's exactly what I want to know."

"Well, I'm sorry to disappoint you. You're barking up the wrong tree. Jenny nagged Dr. Hooper into checking out that transplant stuff. But it seems I'm what they call a bad risk. Too many other problems. They said they wouldn't take me.''

He lit up the cigarette and sighed in satisfaction at the first puff.

Rob shifted in his seat, torn between objecting to what had to be a flagrant violation of Dr. Hooper's orders and a recognition of the other man's freedom of choice. ''Maybe,'' he said, eyeing the cigarette pointedly, ''you could work on clearing up some of those problems and have another evaluation.''

Tate actually shuddered. ''For God's sake, don't say that to Jenny! I wouldn't go through that kind of surgery if *they* offered to pay *me*. I hate hospitals and doctors. I lived my life the way I wanted to, and I'll die the way I want to.''

Rob nodded, accepting Tate's decision with reluctance and regret. The next question he had in mind was even more difficult for him to ask. ''Jenny wouldn't be worried about any other bills, would she, sir?''

''Nope. That girl's always been careful enough for both of us. She nagged me into paying for health insurance when I didn't think I needed to bother with it. Now I'm damned glad she did.''

Once again, Rob had reached a dead end. ''Well, so much for that. I didn't think you could tell me anything, but I had to try.'' He sighed. ''If Jenny was marrying anyone but Keel, maybe I could accept it. But as it is...''

Tate's mouth tautened. ''Keel is a jackass. His father, now there was a man. Frank Keel was a friend you could count on, come good times or bad.''

''He just died a few weeks ago, didn't he?''

"He did. And that fool son of his had him buried in some fancy plot up in Houston." Tate stared at the far wall of the shed as if watching past events replaying themselves on a movie screen. "I went up to see Frank at the hospital the day before he died. He had a dozen tubes and needles in him, and he was out of his head on some damned medication they were feeding him. He didn't even recognize me, but he was babbling to himself a mile a minute about the old days."

Tate brought the cigarette to his mouth for another puff. Then he shifted to look at Rob, his gaze intense. "I don't want to go like that. I want to be in possession of all my faculties, and I want it to happen quick. I'm ready now. The only thing I really mind leaving is Jenny. I'm worried about her. I'd feel a sight easier if she was marrying you. Always figured she would."

"Yeah. Well, so did I."

Tate nodded in empathy. "Who can understand women? My Mary was in love with that no good bastard Parker at one time. God knows why. Everyone knew he was trash."

"From what I hear, you ran him off. He never showed his face in these parts again, did he?"

Rob had expected a long, drawn-out account, Tate's favored style when reminiscing about the good old days. But Tate just tapped the ash from the end of his cigarette and summed it up in a single sentence. "I made sure he wouldn't bother Mary any more."

A minute of silence went by before Rob realized that Tate wasn't going to elaborate. "You'll have to tell me how you managed that, sir," he said half seriously. "Maybe it'll work on Keel."

The sound of an approaching car engine brought the conversation to an abrupt halt.

"Damnation!" Tate hastily rubbed his cigarette out on the edge of the worktable and slipped the unsmoked portion into his pocket.

He shook a warning finger at Rob as the engine sound grew louder, then ceased. "Don't you tell Jenny about my smoking. The girl doesn't give me a minute's peace as it is. After my first heart attack, she hired a woman to do my cooking and cleaning and nag me about my medicine. She threatened to quit school and come home to take care of me herself if I didn't agree to it. Now she thinks I'm doing good, so don't you go getting her all worked up again, y'hear?"

Before Rob could even formulate a reply, Jenny was walking through the doorway.

"Hello, Daddy. They had a sale on boots at Elmer's, and I got..." Her voice trailed away as she narrowed her eyes and sniffed the air. "Daddy, tell me you haven't been smoking again!"

"I haven't been smoking again," Tate said obligingly.

"Daddy, you..." Her eyes finally adjusted to the light, and she saw the other man sitting on the chair near her father.

Fear, humiliation, anger, hope. The emotions surged through her, fighting for supremacy, threatening to tear her apart. How many times would he keep coming back for more? How long could she hold up against his repeated assaults on her weakening defenses? The answer that came to her was unwelcome, but predictable. She would hold out as long as necessary. There was no other alternative.

She wanted to turn and run. Run so fast and so far that exhaustion would blot out every thought, every feeling. But she couldn't even do that. Feeling as if she'd shatter at any moment, she faced Rob squarely. "I didn't see Brandy outside."

"She's around back." Rob got to his feet, all his attention focused on her face, her voice. She looked even thinner than she had the day before, the violet shadows beneath her eyes a shade deeper.

He walked forward and tried to take her arm, but she moved out of his reach. "I think," he said, "we need to talk."

Jenny nodded, both dreading the confrontation, and eager to get it over with. The strain of trying to repress her true feelings, of deceiving those she cared about, was taking a greater toll with each passing day. Each time she saw Rob, another chink appeared in the already too thin armor she wore around her heart. She could feel it crumbling bit by bit. Soon it would be gone, and she would be defenseless.

She couldn't allow that to happen. Her wedding was on Saturday. Surely she could last that long. If only Rob would give up! His persistence was the source of her greatest comfort—and her greatest torment.

Leading the way out into the sunlight, she was determined to steel her heart against him. Then she turned and looked into his eyes. The longing she saw there was so accurate a reflection of her own that it pierced through her like a knife.

She turned away from him, her voice as sharp as the pain she was feeling. "You have no right to come here, no right to upset my father. He's not well. He's—"

"He's worried about you, just like I am."

His hand closed over her shoulder and she shut her eyes, fighting the surge of warmth his touch always inspired. But this time, she couldn't force herself to move away.

Rob stepped up behind her, slowly closing the distance between them until he was snug against her. His arms went around her waist, his cheek nestled against her hair.

"I'm sorry about what happened at the creek, Jen. All day we were working together, sharing things the way we used to. I got to thinking about the future we'd always talked about—a life together on the land, children. It wasn't that I didn't want what you were offering. It was just that I'd hoped for so much more."

Jenny struggled to harden her heart, struggled to find a response. "I—I understand. I have your T-shirt and your thermos—"

He didn't let her finish. He hadn't come this far to let her sidetrack him again. "Listen, Jenny, I talked to my brother today. He and Maggie are going to sign half of the Diamond over to me. I can sell my share and have enough to do anything, to go anywhere I please."

As the meaning of his words penetrated, Jenny's eyes flew open and she turned in his arms. "Sell the land? But, Rob, you can't! You'd be miserable anywhere else."

"I'll be even more unhappy without you."

A moan ripped its way up through Jenny's chest. She grabbed his shirt in both hands. "No! I'd never let you do that to yourself."

"It's not your decision. It's mine, and I've already made it. You said you wanted money. Now I can get all that you need."

Jenny laid her forehead on his shoulder and sagged against his chest in defeat. "I'm not marrying Jack because of his money, Rob. It was all a lie."

Rob smiled slightly and planted a kiss on tresses that seemed to glint with fire in the sunlight. She had confirmed what his heart had known from the beginning. He would have sold the ranch if it had come to that, but he was glad it wouldn't be necessary. He only hoped the truth was as simple to deal with as the lie had been.

One hand beneath her chin, he lifted her face. "Then why *are* you marrying, Keel, Jenny? No matter what the reason is, you can tell me."

Her heart aching for absolution, tears standing in her eyes, Jenny shook her head. "No, I can't."

Rob held her with the intensity of his gaze alone. In a flash, he saw his mother's face, heard his mother's voice. *There are many reasons a woman might feel she has to marry a man. Be sure that you consider all of them.*

Suddenly he knew what his mother had been trying to tell him. The thought made him go cold inside. It seemed so far out of the realm of possibility that he hadn't even considered it. But he'd eliminated everything else.

"Jenny, are you carrying Keel's baby? Because if you are, it doesn't matter. I'll marry you, anyway. It'll be my child. Yours and mine."

He hadn't been quite sure what he'd say until he'd heard the words. He hadn't known just how very much Jenny meant to him. Now he did. And so did she.

He watched as a single tear escaped from her brimming eyes and traced its way down one pale cheek. He wiped it away and pressed his warm lips to hers. Hers were ice-cold and trembling. "Don't cry, sweetheart. There's nothing to cry about anymore. We'll get married right away, and then we'll go to Keel together. We—''

Jenny pressed her fingers to his lips to stop the flow of words—the words that were tearing her soul apart. "Oh, Rob," she whispered. "I never thought that any man could love me so completely, so unselfishly. Or that I'd have to send that man away."

The sense of rightness and completeness Rob had been feeling vanished in an instant. He brushed her fingers aside and grabbed her wrists. "What are you saying, Jenny?"

"I'm not pregnant with Jack's baby, Rob. I've never slept with him or any other man. And I can't marry you."

The hurt and frustration her words inspired were all but unbearable. "You don't love me?"

Jenny looked into his eyes and knew she couldn't go on lying. Not to him. Not anymore. "I've loved you since I was twelve years old, Rob. No one and nothing will ever change that. But I have to marry Keel. I wish I could tell you why, but—'' Her words ended in a gasp as Rob used his hold on her wrists to pull her up on her toes.

A primitive possessiveness rushed through him, threatening to take control. For that brief instant he had only one thought, only one purpose. To keep Jenny for himself no matter what the method, no matter what the cost. If that meant taking her away by force, by God, he'd do it and worry about the consequences later.

"Rob, you're hurting me!"

He looked down at his hands as if they belonged to a stranger. Then he released her and slowly backed away. He stood there breathing deeply, trembling from the adrenaline coursing through his system.

Searching Jenny's features, he was as much at a loss as he had been the day she'd first called him from college to tell him that it was all over between them. This was Jenny, his love and his childhood friend. She had always been the one to reason things out before she acted. The most thoughtful, logical girl he knew. The perfect balance for his impulsiveness. But this time he could see no logic to her actions, no purpose to what she was doing. He could only assume, knowing Jenny, that there was a good one.

"You told me a few days ago, Jen, that I had been the one to let things ride, the one who hadn't been ready to make a commitment. But, you know, the more I think about it, the more I recall that you were the one who drew the line first."

"Me?" Jenny squeaked.

"Yes, you. If you had agreed to sleep with me, I would have been faithful to you until hell froze over. But you didn't trust enough in my love to risk that much of yourself. Even yesterday when you finally offered to make love to me, it was only your body you wanted to give, not your whole heart."

Jenny opened her mouth to protest, but he didn't give her a chance.

"That's the minimum I'll settle for, Jenny. That's what I offered you today, unconditional love, unconditional acceptance. No matter what you've done, it doesn't matter. I want you, anyway. If, knowing that, you can't even trust me enough to tell me what the problem is, then there was never any hope for us. None at all."

Jenny watched him turn away and knew it was for the last time. She wanted to call after him, to give him what he'd asked for. But that was the one thing she couldn't do.

Her eyes misted with tears, she stared after him as he rode up the hill. Then he reached the top and disappeared from view and from her life forever.

Chapter Seven

Rob finished injecting the medicine into the steer's eye and stuck a temporary protective patch in place. Then he hurried back to Brandy and moved her forward to put some slack in the rope that encircled the steer's neck.

The pressure that had held it in place gone, the steer lifted its head and tried to rise. The leather strap that bound three of its feet together prevented it from doing so.

Rob pulled the neck rope free, coiled it up, and returned it to its place on the saddle. He was walking back to pull off the tie that bound the steer's feet when the animal decided to save him the trouble. Struggling free of its bonds on its own, the half-blind steer lurched upright and charged forward. It struck Rob a glancing blow and knocked him flat on his back.

He didn't even have the breath to manage a decent curse. Blinking up at the afternoon sky, he watched it whirl in lazy circles above him. He tried to muster the resolve to get back on his feet, but he didn't seem to have the energy or the inclination.

Jenny was getting married tomorrow. Since he'd left her out at her ranch the day before yesterday, he'd tried his best to work himself into exhaustion, to make himself too tired to think about what had happened—and what was going to happen in less than twenty-four hours. All he'd managed to do was make himself tired enough to be careless on the job.

Even during the few hours of sleep he had managed to steal, Jenny had continued to haunt his thoughts. His dreams had been dark and confused. Nightmares in which he'd been blindfolded and bound hand and foot. He'd heard Jenny calling his name, begging him to help her, but he hadn't even been able to see what was threatening her.

The sky finally stopped spinning just as a large, warm muzzle appeared to block out his view. Brandy dipped her head down and sniffed at his face inquiringly.

"Yeah, I'm still breathing. Not that that's saying a hell of a lot."

He pushed the mare's face aside and got to his feet. Stooping to retrieve his hat, he again fought the urge to ride over to the Landon place, to try to talk to Jenny just one more time. But he knew that he wouldn't. He had offered her everything he had to give, and it hadn't been enough. Unless she changed her mind, there was nothing left to say.

He was slapping the dust out of his jeans when he saw Will in the distance, coming toward him at an all-out gallop. A cold feeling started in his stomach and spread through the rest of his body. Grabbing the reins, he swung into the saddle and spurred Brandy forward. Within seconds, he was hauling up beside Will's sweat-dappled gelding.

"It's Resolute, Rob! She's having trouble breathing. No one's ever seen anything like it."

Rob's hands tightened on the reins, and Brandy danced in place, sensing his agitation. "Not Resolute," he whispered, hardly realizing he'd spoken aloud. Jude had paid a fortune for the brood mare. If they lost her now...

Realizing that every second counted, Rob urged Brandy into a gallop, leaving Will to follow as he would.

Minutes later, he dismounted in the ranch yard and ran toward the main barn. Jesse was in the stall with the stricken mare, speaking to her in a low voice, trying to soothe her.

Rob doubted the animal even heard him. Resolute was staring straight ahead at nothing, her gaze dull and fixed, as if she had to concentrate all her energy on drawing each breath. Saliva dripped from the mare's mouth into the straw that cushioned the bottom of the stall, and the sound of her labored breathing seemed to fill the barn.

Jesse looked up at Rob, clearly near panic. "I don't know what to do! I ain't never heard a horse breathe like this!"

Rob didn't have the heart to tell the man that he hadn't, either. Fighting to control his own fear, he moved to Resolute's head and ran his hand down the length of her throat. "She's not swallowing, but I don't feel anything stuck in there. Is Dr. Meyer on his way?"

Jesse shook his head. "Will called him, but he's way out at the Lazy J finishing up a cesarean on one of their heifers. He said he'd get here as fast as he could."

"That won't be fast enough." Rob knew he'd run out of options. He knew what had to be done. Briefly, he considered sending Jesse to make the call, but that would have been the coward's way out. Despite the emotional consequences, this was something he had to do himself.

Moving quickly, he crossed the ranch yard, entered the kitchen, and dialed her number. She answered on the third ring.

"Hello?"

He fought against the warm feeling that rushed through him at the sound of her voice. Even now, with just one word, she had the power to stir him.

"Jenny, I've got a mare who's having trouble breathing and swallowing. I've never seen anything this bad. Dr. Meyer's not going to get here in time."

There was a brief hesitation, a silence filled with a pain that mirrored his own. Then, "I'm on my way."

The dial tone echoed in his ear. He stood there, hating himself for being glad that an emergency had given him the chance to see her just one more time. Even knowing that seeing her again would be agony, that it would change nothing, he craved the contact like an alcoholic longing for just one more drink. But he didn't have the time for either self-analysis or regrets.

Forcing everything out of his mind but the situation at hand, he hung up the phone and started back to the barn. If this mare died, his brother's hopes for his breeding program died with her. He couldn't shake the feeling that he was somehow responsible. His

brother had left him in charge, but he'd been so
wrapped up in Jenny that somehow, somewhere, he'd
missed something.

As Rob entered the barn he saw that Will was there
with Jesse now, both men looking on helplessly. Rob
approached the stall with a feeling of doom. Resolute
looked even worse than she had moments before. She
was still laboring for breath, still drooling. And now
she was swaying on her feet.

Rob said a silent prayer—for his brother's hopes
and for the beautiful animal slowly suffocating in
front of his eyes. It seemed like an eternity before the
sound of a car engine drew his gaze toward the doorway.

Jenny jumped out of her Jeep and hurried into the
barn, medical bag in hand. She felt the same pull she
always did at the sight of Rob, but her thoughts
quickly focused on the stricken mare.

The glassy stare, the drooling, the rasping breath,
the trembling legs combined to set off alarm bells in
her mind. She ran her hands along the animal's throat
and felt a flicker of panic when she found nothing out
of the ordinary.

"What is it?" Jesse asked, his voice high and
strained.

Jenny shook her head. "I wish to God I knew."

Quickly, she walked around the animal, checking
for any other symptoms. She felt a surge of triumph
mixed with relief when she discovered the penny-size
bumps scattered across the mare's back and flanks.

"Tell me," Rob demanded, reading her expression.

"It's got to be an allergic reaction of some kind," she told him as she reached into her bag. "Her larynx is so swollen she can't swallow, and the swelling is about to close off the trachea. When that's completely blocked, she won't be able to breathe at all."

"Can you save her?" Rob asked as he watched her fill a syringe.

"I can try."

Jenny located the large jugular vein, wiped the area with disinfectant, and plunged the needle into the animal's neck. "If I'm right, Adrenalin should reverse the swelling. I just don't know if it will work in time."

As if in confirmation of her doubts, Resolute staggered and sank to her knees in the straw. Jesse barely managed to leap out of the way of the flailing hoofs as the animal collapsed onto her side. Seconds later the sound of the labored breathing ceased, and the resulting silence was more terrible than any sound that Rob had ever heard.

"Hold her head!"

Moving to obey Jenny's order, Rob pushed by Jesse and knelt down in the straw. He looked up at her, searching for hope and reassurance, but all her attention was focused on her patient.

Jenny injected a local anesthetic into Resolute's throat, made sure that the necessary tube was within reach, then picked up a scalpel. She brought it against the mare's neck and steeled herself to make the incision.

Then, suddenly, the animal shuddered under her hands and she felt the big chest rise to push against her knee.

She laughed out loud in relief. "She's breathing! The Adrenalin worked! She's breathing."

Stroking the glossy neck that she had come within a heartbeat of laying open, she carefully replaced the unused scalpel in her bag.

Resolute's condition improved rapidly. Within minutes, the drooling stopped and the breathing returned to normal. As if waking from a nap, the mare got her legs under her and stood. She looked around at the four people who were staring at her so intently and pricked her ears forward as if to ask what the fuss was all about. Then, obviously dismissing them, she dropped her head and began to munch on a morsel of hay.

Will shook his head in amazement. "I just don't believe it!"

Jenny used her stethoscope to check the animal's heart and lungs, her hands shaking slightly with reaction now that the crisis was over. "The Adrenalin did its work. Now that the swelling's down, she should be fine."

A little giddy with relief himself, Rob came over to stand beside her. "But what caused it? Will it happen again?"

"It's hard to say with these things. There are tests that I—" She caught herself in midsentence and Rob watched as all the vitality and enthusiasm seemed to fade from her face and her voice. "There are tests that Dr. Meyer can run."

Rob turned and gave Jesse and Will a pointed look. Will cleared his throat. "Well, I guess we'll...uh, go on and call Doc Meyer and tell him not to bother comin'."

"Good idea," Rob responded. He watched the two ranch hands walk out of the barn, then turned back to

Jenny. "How can you give this up, Jenny? This is what you were meant to do, and you know it."

Jenny looked out into the fast-approaching darkness and knew the time had come to be honest with him and with herself. "Yes, I know it. I also know that it's something I can't have. Just like I can't have you."

She looked at him and gave him a ghost of a smile. "I thought about what you said the last time I saw you, about me holding back and being afraid of commitment. You were right. I didn't trust in your love for me. I always thought of myself as the ugly duckling in love with the handsome prince. I couldn't believe you would ever love me as much as I loved you. I was wrong."

Rob took a step toward her, hope welling up despite what she'd said before. But before he could speak, she was already shaking her head. "No, please, don't say anything, because nothing you say can change things. I still can't make any promises. I just wanted you to know that I love you, Rob. I love you with all my heart. And I want to stay with you tonight. I want to give you the only thing I have left to give you."

Turning away from her, Rob faced the darkness. He felt enough anger and frustration to want to slam his fist into the wall. And he felt the hurt of her rejection. If he took her now, that pain would be unbearable tomorrow. But had he been a fool to refuse her before? Wasn't having her for one night better than not having her at all?

She had admitted that she loved him. If he was letting his guard down and opening himself up to hurt, then so was she. Making love to her was the best chance he'd ever have to change her mind. It was the only chance.

Jenny watched him turn back to her and read his decision in his eyes. If she'd had any sense, she would have turned and fled. Far from temptation, far from the pain she knew would be hers in the morning. But the pain would be there, anyway. Tomorrow and for the rest of her life. Tonight would give her one memory to cherish, one hour of happiness in a lifetime of despair.

Letting her medical bag drop to the floor, Jenny walked toward Rob. He met her halfway and they gazed at each other in the fading light. Then, slowly, Rob lowered his mouth to hers. His lips moved over hers, caressed hers, eased hers open for the gentle invasion of his tongue.

Putting her arms around his neck, Jenny stood on tiptoe, straining toward him, hungry for his touch.

Rob felt the passion of her response and was nearly swept away by it. But he fought against its lure. Tonight was for Jenny. Tonight was the last chance he had to make her his, body and soul.

His muscles trembling with restraint, he ran his hands down over her body in possession and promise. Then he put an arm under her knees and swung her feet off the floor.

Jenny felt as if she were floating on air as Rob carried her to a vacant stall in the back of the barn. On the way, his mouth dipped to hers for several quick, ardent kisses, as if he couldn't bear to forgo the taste of her for even the short length of their journey.

Then they were falling into the shadows, into the sweet-smelling straw, holding each other tightly as they rolled over once, and then again.

Rob covered the flushed skin of her face and neck with kisses, his hands shaking as they undid the buttons of her blouse. One round blue disk went skittering into the straw before he managed to complete the task. With fingers that had always been sure before, he fumbled with the front clasp of her bra. Then, all at once, she was his.

Sliding one arm beneath her back, he arched her up toward him. Then, with a soft sigh of anticipation, he lowered his head.

The first touch of his tongue sent shivers through her. As he drew her into his mouth, she writhed beneath him, drowning in a sea of sensation. Desperate to touch him in turn, she grabbed the back of his shirt and pulled it free. Running her hands up underneath the sweat-damp material, she traced the smooth, strong muscles of his back. Then she felt them bunch under her hands as he lifted himself away from her.

Feeling abandoned, she tried to pull him back, but he only shook his head. Sitting up, he pulled off first her boots, then his own. When he'd completed that task, he unfastened her jeans and tugged both jeans and panties down over her thighs and feet.

Unwilling to waste time on buttons, Jenny dragged his shirt over his head, and reached down to open the snap on his jeans.

Then, suddenly, they were mouth to mouth, flesh to flesh, heart to heart. Jenny felt him trembling, felt his battle for restraint in every cell of her body. She moved to wrap her legs around him, to make their union complete. But he wouldn't allow it.

Twisting free, he moved down her body, licking, caressing, taking her inch by throbbing inch. His hands slipped beneath her bottom, cupping, squeezing, raising her for the most intimate kiss of all.

All the air seemed to leave Jenny's lungs as she gasped at the intensity of the pleasure he was giving her. She lifted her head and looked down at him, down to where the shining black of his hair mingled with the dark red of hers. The hopelessly erotic sight took away her last inhibition.

She reached down and threaded her fingers through those midnight locks, trying to draw him closer, trying to find release from the terrible tension that was growing inside her. The tension that was transforming her body into a coiled spring.

His hands moved over her hips and his palms slid upward, tracing twin pathways across her belly and her rib cage to the sensitive tips of her breasts. His fingers traced the hard, velvet beads, caressed them, closed around them.

A trembling began in the deepest part of Jenny's body. A trembling that radiated outward to every cell, every molecule of her being. She cried out his name and wrapped her legs around his shoulders, her hands clutching his head, her heart pounding in time to the contractions pulsing through her.

Rob growled deep in his throat, exultantly, possessively. In this moment she was his undeniably, completely. He rode out the storm, absorbing the essence of her passion, continuing to caress her until her trembling ceased and she lay spent beneath him.

Then, he moved up over her. Brown eyes met gray, communicating wonder, elation, love. And a passion that would never be fully quenched.

Jenny felt a stab of anguish as she realized all that she was giving up, all that she must leave behind. And she knew that the pain would grow even deeper before the night was over. But she could no more have denied herself these last few hours than she could have willed her heart to stop beating.

Fighting back tears, she reached up and drew Rob down toward her. She would take what he had taken, give what he had given. All her tomorrows might belong to another, but tonight she was all his. His and his alone.

"Jenny...Jenny Landon, are you in here?"

Rob and Jenny froze in place as the sound of her name seemed to echo in every corner of the big barn.

"Dr. Meyer!" Jenny whispered. "He must have already been on his way over here when the hands called the Lazy J."

Frantically, she searched out her scattered clothing and dressed faster than she ever had in her life. Hoping that Dr. Meyer would be more concerned with examining Resolute than searching for her, she buttoned all the buttons that remained on her blouse with fingers that shook and fumbled. Then she pulled on her underwear, jeans and boots, and moved to push to her feet.

Catching her arm, Rob held her still and pulled a stray wisp of straw from her hair.

Jenny looked into his eyes and wanted to throw herself right back into his arms. Instead she gave him a whispered promise. "I'll be back."

"And I'll be waiting." He kissed her, hard, hot and deep, then settled back into the straw with a sigh that was equal parts frustration and anticipation.

Checking the fastenings on her clothes one final time, Jenny gathered her courage and walked out of the stall. She followed the sound of Dr. Meyer's voice to the front of the barn.

The elderly vet had his back toward her and was murmuring to Resolute reassuringly as he examined the mare.

"How does she look?" Jenny asked, trying to sound casual.

Dr. Meyer started visibly and turned to look at her in reproach. "Resolute is fine. I, on the other hand, have just lost ten years off my life. Ten years that I cannot afford! Don't you know it's not polite to go sneaking around scaring old veterinarians?"

Jenny smiled at her old mentor and offered an apology. But her smile faded at his next comment.

"So, Jenny, you're still determined to move away to Houston. I can't believe that you won't be the one who takes over my practice."

Her heart sinking, Jenny covered the same ground she had at Jude's wedding when she had first broken the news of her change in career plans to Dr. Meyer.

Once again the older vet tried to change her mind. By the time she had sidetracked him into a discussion of Resolute's case, the sky outside was dark and spangled with stars.

Dr. Meyer was still shaking his head when she finally succeeded in herding him to his car. "Jenny, my girl, I think you're going to regret this decision."

Jenny watched him drive away, knowing that she already did. But she still had tonight.

Feeling both apprehension and anticipation, she made her way back to the stall where she'd left Rob. She entered the small enclosure, then came to a halt, staring down at him in disbelief.

He was still lying as she had left him, sprawled in the straw. He was bare-chested, the snap of his jeans unfastened, a half smile on his lips. A very enticing picture, except for one small detail—he was fast asleep.

A reluctant smile curved her lips as she gazed at him. He looked like a little boy. So innocent. So vulnerable.

Sinking to a sitting position in the straw, she reached out and brushed a stray lock of hair from his forehead. "My love," she whispered, yearning for all that had been denied her. Yearning for what would never be, could never be.

But maybe it was just as well that she hadn't known the full extent of this man's possession. Would she still have been able to walk away from him after that? She didn't want to know the answer.

The reckless courage that had come to her earlier had fled to parts unknown. She was afraid of the consequences if she tested her resolve by waking him, by giving herself to him completely. But neither could she bring herself to leave him—not before it was absolutely necessary.

So, in the end, she covered him with an old blanket and settled down nearby to share the final hours of her freedom with him in the only way she dared. And she prayed that morning would never come.

Chapter Eight

"Hold still, girl. I just want to take a good look at you."

At the sound of his brother's voice, Rob's eyes drifted open. He blinked in the morning sunlight, confused and disoriented.

What was he doing waking up half naked in an empty horse stall? Then he remembered, and all the light seemed to go out of the day.

Feeling the cold hand of panic clutching at his heart, he pushed aside the blanket that had been draped over him and pulled on his shirt and boots.

He came barreling out of the enclosure like a racehorse from the starting gate and found Jude standing by Resolute's stall.

His brother looked up from stroking the mare's glossy neck and gave him an understanding look. "Slow down, *hermano*. Jenny's not getting married for a couple of hours yet."

Rob ran his fingers through his hair, feeling the bite of fear lessen for the moment. Then despair came rushing in to fill the gap. He crossed to the doorway and gazed out at the ranch yard unseeingly.

"What's the difference?" he said with a shrug. "Even if she's not married now, she will be before the day is over."

A part of him still didn't want to accept that fact. But how could he deny it any longer? If she could leave him after what they'd shared last night—leave him without even saying goodbye—then that was the end. He'd taken his best shot, and he'd lost.

Feeling a sudden chill in the warm air, he shoved his hands into his pockets and turned back toward his brother. "How did you ... uh, get here from the airport?" he asked a little guiltily.

"Will was there waiting for us at the gate. He said to tell you he was returning the favor. Does that mean anything to you?"

Despite the gloomy prospects for the day, Rob smiled. "It means he's a better friend than I deserve."

Jude walked over to stand beside his brother. He frowned in concentration, obviously considering his words carefully. "Jenny was here when I got in. She said she sat up with Resolute all night—just to make sure everything was okay."

"We both did," Rob said, his eyes daring Jude to challenge that statement.

Jude looked toward the vacant stall and let out a breath of air. "I'm on your side," he said, his voice a soft reprimand. "If there was anything I could do to change things, I would."

"You've done enough already by offering me a share of the ranch. It didn't change anything. The woman has her mind made up."

"That's what she said. Didn't seem too happy about it, though."

Rob nodded. "That hasn't stopped her so far."

"You going to the wedding?"

Rob forced himself to consider the question. He wanted to get in his pickup and just drive. He wanted to run away from the hurt, to start over again some place where no one knew what had happened and no one cared.

But the Diamond was here and his family was here. And there was a streak of mule-stubborn determination inside him that said it wasn't over till it was over.

Fumbling for the right words, pausing frequently, he tried to tell his brother how he felt. "My common sense tells me to stay clear, to let her go. But I know she loves me, Jude. If she has the gall to stand up in front of God and Layton City and pledge herself to another man, then she's going to have to have the guts to do it in front of me, too. I won't let her hide. I won't let her think I've given up on us."

He looked at Jude, at the one man left whose opinion mattered to him. "Does that make me weak? Some men might say so. But I don't feel weak, Jude. I feel stronger than I ever have before."

His brother met his questioning gaze and gave him an answer that came from the heart. "You're the only judge that counts, Rob. I was afraid to take a chance on Maggie, and I almost lost her because of it. I don't think it's weak to lay your heart on the line, little brother. I happen to know that it takes a hell of a man to bet it all."

Jude's answer quieted Rob's last lingering doubt. The pain of watching Jenny's wedding might slice his heart in two, but she was going to have to see that pain in his eyes and get past it. She was going to have to walk over him to get to Keel.

With a nod to his brother, Rob left the barn and walked toward his mother's house, toward a hot shower and a fresh set of clothes. And toward whatever destiny lay in wait for him.

Jenny straightened her veil and looked into her dresser mirror. She saw violet shadows no makeup could cover, a weariness that no amount of sleep could ease.

She'd been up all night, checking on Resolute periodically. But most of the time she'd spent just watching Rob sleep.

She'd been afraid to close her eyes. Afraid that when she opened them, morning would have come and she would have lost the only time she had left to spend with him.

So she had simply watched him, trying not to think of the future, allowing herself to draw a measure of comfort from his nearness.

But eventually, the morning had come, anyway. She didn't know how she would have found the strength to get up—to leave Rob after what they'd shared—if Jude hadn't come into the barn to examine Resolute. Even then, the parting had left her heart an open wound.

Talking to Jude, she'd related what had happened with the mare. All the while, she'd moved closer to her car, determined to make her escape before he could raise any other, more personal topic.

She'd breathed a sigh of relief as she had slipped behind the steering wheel. But that feeling had been premature. Jude had leaned down and looked at her with those dark eyes that were so like Rob's and asked her right out if she still intended to marry Keel.

She'd barely managed to mumble a yes, start the engine, and get the Jeep headed down the driveway before the tears had filled her eyes. But she hadn't let them fall. Not yet.

She still felt as if a part of herself—the most important part—had been left behind in that barn with Rob. She felt numb, as if she were in a trance. As if she were just going through the motions.

A tapping on her bedroom door returned her thoughts to the present. Lissa appeared behind her in the mirror, clad in a pink matron of honor's dress.

Their gazes locked in the glass and held for a long moment. But in the end, all Lissa said was, "It's time."

Her stomach jumping nervously, Jenny forced herself to get to her feet. All she had to do was get through the next few minutes, and then it would all be over. She'd be Jack's wife. There'd be no more soul-searching, no chance of turning back. She was strong enough to see it through. She had to be.

Rob crested the hill overlooking the Landon ranch and reined Brandy to a halt. Shifting in the saddle, he stared down at the scene below.

The guests were standing in groups behind the rows of neatly arranged folding chairs, the women's dresses forming a kaleidoscope of color against the green backdrop of the lawn. They were sipping drinks and talking as if this were any other day, any other wedding. To them, it was a celebration, a beginning. To Rob, it was the end of everything.

He let his mind drift back over the events of the past week, replaying them, analyzing his actions. But there was nothing he would have done differently, nothing he'd left unsaid.

His attention was drawn back to the guests, and he realized that they were beginning to file to their seats. The Reverend Thatcher, Keel and Travis moved to the end of the red-carpeted aisle to stand under the sheltering canopy that had been erected there.

The wedding march began to play, and Lissa Jackson appeared in the back doorway of the ranch house, bouquet in hand. She negotiated the steps like the former beauty queen she was and glided down the aisle in time to the music, clearly enjoying her moment in the spotlight.

Rob held his breath, waiting for Jenny to show herself. The seconds crawled by and, suddenly, she was there in the doorway, holding fast to Tate's arm.

Concentrating all his thoughts, Rob willed her to look his way. She was approaching the back porch steps when he got his wish. She looked toward him and froze in place, teetering on the edge of that first step, almost falling before Tate steadied her.

She held his gaze for one heart-stopping second. Then, with a jerk of her head, she broke the tenuous contact and completed her descent to the yard.

Rob felt his last hope die. His jaw clenched, and Brandy danced beneath him. Jenny belonged to him! He was only a breath away from riding down the hill and carrying her away—whether she was willing or not. A hundred years ago, he could have. Now, convention bound him. Convention and love. A love that

acknowledged Jenny's innate right to choose another. He respected that right, but he didn't have to
like it.

Defiantly, he held his place as the audience turned
to watch Jenny's approach. He saw the pointing fingers, could almost hear the startled whispers as, one
by one, the spectators noticed him on the hill.

He didn't give a tinker's damn who pointed or who
laughed. All his attention was focused on Jenny. With
everything that was in him, with all the love he felt, he
willed her to change her mind.

Jenny stood before the preacher, hearing the sound
of his voice, but unable to concentrate on the words.
She saw only the scene that was indelibly etched on her
brain. Rob waiting on the hill above, trying to draw
her to him by the sheer strength of his love.

Feelings coursed through her, battling for supremacy: her loathing for Jack, her love for her father, her
need for Rob. All at once she knew she'd been wrong.
The marriage ceremony wouldn't end anything. The
pain wouldn't be over. It would just be beginning.

She would see Rob's face, just as she was seeing it
now, for the rest of her life. It would haunt her every
time Jack made love to her, and it would be reflected
in the eyes of the children that should have been
Rob's. Even as she lay dying, Rob's face would be the
last sight in her mind's eye.

"If anyone knows why these two people should not
be joined in holy wedlock, let him speak now or forever hold his peace."

Rob's shout rang out over the crowd, as loud and
clear as the blast of a bugle sounding a call to arms. "I
love you, Jenny Landon!"

There was a wave of sound as the crowd broke into open conversation and again turned in their chairs to stare at the horseman on the hill.

Jenny looked from Jack's anger-flushed face to her father's hopeful expression, then, finally, to the grimly determined set of Rob's jaw. She could no longer deny it. The boy she'd loved had grown up at last. He'd made a commitment to her—and he'd put his pride on the line by doing it in front of everyone in Layton City. Despite her repeated rejections, despite the consequences, he had risked everything for her.

She saw what happened next as if it were happening to someone else and she were a spectator watching. She saw the wedding bouquet falling from her hands. Then she saw her arms rising slowly, slowly, as she held them out toward the man she loved.

The fragile restraint that had been holding Rob in check vanished as if it had never been. A wild feeling of triumph coursed through him as he spurred his mount forward. The roan mare cantered down the hill, gathering momentum as she went.

Rob saw a blurred sea of color and faces as he rode Brandy down the aisle. His mother was staring at him and smiling, tears of joy in her eyes. Jude was laughing and hugging Maggie. Todd was watching open-mouthed, his eyes wide as saucers. The ranch hands were on their feet cheering, and Will threw his hat in the air and let loose with a rebel yell.

As Rob pulled up at the end of the aisle, he caught a glimpse of Tate, yelling encouragement, waving him on. Then, suddenly, a huge form loomed up and grabbed his reins.

Brandy whinnied sharply and back-stepped, trying to escape the man holding her head. He hung on tenaciously, reaching up for the rider on her back. But Rob hadn't come this far to be stopped now.

He pulled one foot free of the stirrup, planted it in the middle of Travis's broad chest and pushed. The big man lost his grip on the reins and fell to the ground.

He was trying to rise when a hundred and twelve pounds of taffeta-clad female delivered a blow with her pink high- heeled shoe that rolled his eyes back in his head. Travis curled up into a moaning ball as Lissa grinned up at Rob and gave him a thumbs-up sign.

Urging Brandy forward, Rob ran head-on into a red-faced and furious Jack Keel. Sweating and cursing, the man attempted to grab onto Rob's denim jacket. Rob turned Brandy abruptly, dislodging Keel and sending him catapulting into the front row of guests.

Then, suddenly, there was only Jenny. Rob leaned down and slipped an arm around her waist. She reached up to clasp his neck, and he pulled her awkwardly across his lap.

He glanced down at the elderly Reverend Thatcher, who was clutching his prayer book and blinking up at them through his thick-lensed glasses. "I'm sure sorry about all this, Reverend."

Seeing Keel coming at him again, Rob didn't wait for a reply. He clucked to Brandy and lifted the reins. The mare seemed more than eager to leave the confusion and excitement behind. With a toss of her head, she took off at a dead run. Rob grabbed one of the poles as they passed, dislodging it and bringing the canopy down on top of Travis, Keel and the hapless minister.

To Rob, time seemed to take on a new quality that day. It was measured in hoofbeats and the growing distance that separated them from what they had left behind.

He purposely chose a path that even a Jeep would have difficulty following—though he doubted anyone would try. It wasn't as if he'd carried Jenny off against her will. She'd *chosen* him.

As he held his woman in his arms and bore her onto his land, he felt a possessiveness as primitive as first man's. Exhilaration rushed through him. He wanted to ride on forever, cherishing the sweet contentment that came with holding her against his heart and knowing that she was finally his. But he knew that she must be growing tired and uncomfortable, despite her lack of complaint.

Minutes later, he reined up in a secluded glade where soft green grass and wildflowers flourished in the shelter of the surrounding trees. The setting and his feelings seemed older than time itself.

He pushed off the mare, then reached up for Jenny. His hands on her waist, he steadied her as she all but fell from the saddle, holding her poised above him for endless seconds as he gazed into her gray eyes.

He had expected to see a transcendent happiness to equal his own. Instead he saw only remorse and desperation.

"I have to go back!" she told him. "I *have* to."

All the warmth seemed to drain from Rob's body, and his victory became a hollow, meaningless thing. She was talking as if she'd had nothing to do with the decision to leave Keel at the altar, as if what had happened was all his fault. For an instant he wondered if he could have wanted a signal from her so desperately that he'd imagined something that had never happened. But he wasn't given to self-justifying illusions no matter what the provocation. Her response hadn't been only in his imagination. The guilt in her eyes was all too real.

He saw it, recognized it, and felt it call up a protectiveness and a caring that no anger could fully extinguish.

Lowering Jenny to her feet, he released her trembling body and took a step backward, willing to give her the space she so obviously needed. "There's no going back," he said, knowing he spoke the truth. "When you held out your arms to me, you made your choice and you know it. Now don't you think it's about time you told me what's wrong?"

Even through the fog of exhaustion and the pressure of nerves stripped raw by weeks of constant tension, Jenny could see that he was right.

In leaving Jack, she had acted on pure instinct and emotion. She'd followed her heart and ridden away with Rob despite the cost. There was no way to undo what she'd done. Not now. Not ever.

Like a marionette whose strings had suddenly been cut, she dropped to a sitting position on the grass.

Rob moved to help her, but she held up a restraining hand. What she had to say was hard enough. If he touched her, if he offered her any sympathy, she felt that her tenuous control might shatter into so many pieces that she'd never be able to pull it together again. The least she owed him before that happened was a coherent explanation, some justification for all the hell she'd put him through—that she'd put them both through. And she wanted and needed the release that sharing her secret with him would bring.

Taking a deep breath, she began to speak. "Jack Keel came to see me at school a few weeks ago. I was stunned when he asked me to marry him. Since I had never even agreed to a date with the man, I couldn't imagine what he was thinking of. I turned him down—politely. Then he smiled that nasty smile of his and told me why I was going to agree to his proposal."

Rob felt the tension seeping from her body into his. He wished he'd taken the time earlier to beat Keel to a pulp. But he restrained the urge to tell Jenny so. There would be time later to vent his anger. Now he wanted to hear the rest of her story.

"Jack's father, Frank Keel, had been a friend of Daddy's for years. Just before Frank died, he was out of his head from the medication and the pain. Jack told me he was visiting the hospital room, hardly listening as his father rambled on about the old days. Then, suddenly, he heard Daddy's name and the word murder."

Rob felt as if he'd been hit by an unseen opponent from a direction where he'd thought no danger lurked. "Murder?" he said, his tone incredulous. "Tate?"

Jenny had thought herself immune to those words, had thought she'd come to terms with them weeks ago. But somehow Rob had triggered an emotional flashback to the shock and denial she'd experienced when Jack had first confronted her.

She shuddered at the memory of the gloating look on his face as he'd talked about his father's last moments and her father's crime. The lust in his eyes as he'd put one sweaty palm on her knee and leaned close to whisper the words that had torn her world apart.

Even now she had to struggle to overcome the nausea and the shame that welled up inside her. "For

years everyone believed that Tate chased my natural
father, Leroy Parker, out of the area. But Jack told me
his father saw Daddy shoot Leroy in cold blood and
bury the body in an unmarked grave. Jack said he
knew where Leroy's body was buried. That he'd go to
Sheriff Dawson and have the body and the bullet it
contained exhumed unless I agreed to marry him."

Tate's words about Leroy Parker came back to Rob
in the silent glade. *I made sure he wouldn't bother
Mary anymore.* Trying to ignore the shiver that raced
up his spine, he concentrated on making sense of Jenny's revelation. "And you believed Keel's story? How
do you know he didn't make the whole thing up?"

Jenny shook her head, remembering how it had
been. "I did call Jack a liar. I slapped his face and told
him to leave. He just laughed at me and told me that
if I doubted what he'd said, I could just call home and
ask Daddy about it."

"And did you?" Rob asked, wondering what part
Tate had played in all of this. He couldn't picture the
man trading his daughter to Keel to save his own hide.
Besides, Tate had told him that he was as much in the
dark about Jenny's motives for marrying Keel as he
himself was. And he'd never known Tate to lie.

"I never got that far," Jenny confessed. "My hand
was on the phone when an old memory came back to
me. Something from years ago, when I was just a
child."

She pressed her hands together, trying without success to stop their trembling. "Mama was in labor with
the baby she was carrying, and she was in awful pain.
Her screaming woke me up. I thought someone was
hurting her. I ran down the hall to my parents' room
and peeked around the edge of the door. Daddy was

sitting on the bed, stroking her hair and telling her Doc Hooper was on the way. But Mama kept shaking her head. She grabbed his shirt in her hands and said, 'I'm dying, Tate. I know I am. A life for a life. I have to pay for Leroy's life with my own!' "

Jenny clutched the material of her wedding dress in both hands, as she had seen her mother clutch Tate's shirt. The fragile lace tore, but she didn't even notice. "Daddy said, 'It's my debt to pay, Mary, not yours. I'm the one who took his life.' "

Looking up at Rob, she felt as lost as she had weeks ago when the memory had first come back to her. "My mama and the baby she carried died an hour later. I guess I didn't want to remember anything about that day. I guess I'd blocked it out of my mind until Jack's threat brought it all back to me."

Rob felt a growing understanding of just what she'd been through, what she was still going through. He shifted his stance marginally and listened as she continued.

"So many things went through my mind in that dorm room. I thought of confronting Daddy. Finding out which gun he'd used and where the body was buried, and somehow getting rid of the evidence. Anything to protect Daddy and avoid losing you. But even if I could have managed all that with Keel keeping watch on me, there was no way I could even attempt it without my father's cooperation.

"And you know Daddy," she said with a sad, affectionate smile. "He would have turned himself in in a minute if he even suspected that Keel was blackmailing me. Or even if he just found out I knew about the killing. He's always been such a stickler on right and wrong. I know he'd have gone to the sheriff himself before now if he hadn't been responsible for taking care of me."

If she'd been speaking of any other man, Rob might have considered that a naive belief. Yet, when it came to Tate, he had to agree with Jenny's conclusion. It was her assessment of the entire situation that he was having difficulty with.

"But, Jen, surely, considering the time that's passed, Tate's age and the way Parker abused your mama, Tate stands a damned good chance of getting a suspended sentence—or even being let off entirely."

Jenny looked up at him, willing him to understand. "Daddy has a bad heart condition. Even if he were never actually sentenced to prison, the trauma of being questioned about what happened might be enough to bring on an attack—let alone the ordeal of an inquest or a trial. There was no way out, Rob. In the end, even I had to admit that. So I agreed to marry Jack on the condition that he'd never tell Daddy or anyone else about the killing."

Her eyes glittered with unshed tears. "Ever since, I've been torn between the need to protect Daddy and my need for you. In the end, I chose you. Now I just don't know if I can live with the consequences of that choice."

Rob felt an overwhelming surge of relief and optimism. At last, he knew what the problem was. Now they could move to deal with it. To him, the decision was clear and would have been from the first. He thought he understood why Jenny had acted as she had. But it wasn't how he would have handled things.

In his world, a man of any age or state of physical frailty fought his own battles or he ceased to be considered a man. Tate wouldn't have appreciated any-

one trying to do the job for him, and Rob wouldn't
have insulted him by offering to.

Squatting down next to Jenny, he took her cold
hands in his. "You have to tell Tate. You should have
done it from the start. He's a grown man and a pretty
tough one. Killing Parker was his choice, and he'd be
the first one to tell you so. It's his responsibility to decide how to deal with the consequences of his actions."

He looked into her eyes and tried to share his conviction with her. "I'll be there with you, Jenny. I love
you, and I'll be there to stand by you and Tate. No
matter what."

Jenny felt the pull of his love, the lure of the hope
he was holding out to her. Gradually her heart slowed
its fear-induced pounding, her trembling stopped, and
her world settled back into its normal orbit for the first
time since Jack had leeringly revealed the true fate of
her natural father.

Maybe she'd been a fool to let Jack blackmail her.
Maybe everything would turn out all right, after all.
She wanted to believe it would. She *had* to believe it.

"I love you, Robert Emory."

The elation that Rob had been feeling earlier came
rushing back. He would justify the choice Jenny had
made today. He would make things right again for her
and for her father if he had to take on the rest of the
world to accomplish it.

Pulling her to her feet, he slid Keel's engagement
ring from her finger. Her heart soaring despite her
misgivings, she watched as he replaced it with a plain
gold band.

"My daddy gave Mama this ring on their wedding day. It belonged to his mother. This morning Mama gave it to me for good luck. I guess it worked."

He gave her a smile that told her how he felt more clearly than any words.

She smiled right back at him. "It's beautiful, Rob. Just beautiful."

"Not half as beautiful as you." He held the hand with the ring up between them. "For better or for worse," he said, looking deep into her eyes.

Jenny hesitated, thinking of her father, thinking of the consequences. But that decision was behind her now. Now there was only Rob and their future together.

"For better or for worse," she confirmed.

As Rob bent to seal their vow with a kiss, she experienced a sense of rightness, of completeness that nothing could ever change. Whatever might happen, Rob would be there beside her. She wasn't alone anymore.

Chapter Nine

Gathering her courage, Jenny squeezed Rob's hand and opened the door of the ranch house.

"Welcome back," Tate said. Grinning up at them from the living-room rocker, he used the remote control to switch off the evening news. "That was the best damned wedding I ever attended!"

The two men seated on the old leather sofa seemed far less pleased with the afternoon's events.

Travis sipped a cup of coffee and took in the sight of the embroidered Mexican peasant blouse and skirt that Jenny had bought to replace her bedraggled wedding dress. Then he met the warning look Rob directed at him, his big-boned face expressionless.

Keel sprang to his feet and strode toward them. He came to a stop within a foot of where they stood and shook his cigar under Jenny's nose.

"I figured you'd show up here before too long. I

suppose now you're sorry, and you expect me to be generous enough to forgive you?''

Jenny shook her head and held out her hand. She dropped the diamond engagement ring into Keel's jacket pocket. ''It's too late for that, Jack. Rob and I drove across the border to Mexico and got married this afternoon.''

Keel's face flushed and for a moment Jenny thought she saw a flash of genuine pain in his eyes. Then the moment was gone and all she saw there was rage. The rage of a spoiled child who had just been told he wasn't allowed to have a coveted toy.

''Then I guess I'll have to have that talk with your daddy.''

Jenny raised her chin. ''No, but I will.''

Bypassing a clearly astonished Keel, Jenny crossed the room and sank to her knees by her father's chair. She took his gnarled hand in both of hers and looked up into the face she loved so well.

''Daddy, I have something to tell you. But you've got to promise me you won't get upset.''

Tate's eyes narrowed. He looked at her with shadows in his eyes and nodded for her to continue.

Jenny took a deep breath, then pushed ahead as fast as she could, wanting to get the hurting over with. ''On his deathbed, Frank Keel talked about the day he'd seen you and Leroy Parker. About how you'd shot Leroy and buried the body. Jack was in the hospital room and listened to his father's ramblings. After he'd verified the facts, he came to me and threatened to go to the sheriff unless I married him.''

''I never knew,'' Tate said. ''I never knew Frank saw me.'' His eyes filled with tears and he shook his head back and forth. ''And you, Jenny... Knowing I murdered your natural father, you agreed to marry a man like Keel in order to protect me?''

Awkwardly, he pulled her to her feet and onto his lap. He sat rocking her, stroking her hair while her tears soaked his shirt. ''Ah, girl, I can't say I regret killing your father, and I'm willing to pay for what I did. I was just afraid that if you ever found out, you'd surely hate me for it.''

Jenny pulled back to look at his face, smiling through her tears. ''You're my father, not Leroy Parker. And I could never hate you. No matter what.''

''That's all I care about.'' Tate wiped his eyes and glared at Keel, more power and conviction in his voice than Jenny had heard in years. ''All right, Keel, you've had your free show. I would have gone to the sheriff myself a long time ago if it hadn't been for Jenny. Now I don't care who knows. If you want to call Sheriff Dawson, the phone's in the kitchen.''

Fury in every line of his body, Keel turned to take advantage of Tate's offer. When he found Rob blocking his path, he smiled an ugly smile.

''You'd better get out of my way, *Row-bare-toe,* or you're going to be one sorry greaseball.''

Rob clenched his fists and smiled. ''Not as sorry as you're going to be when I get through with you, you bigoted bastard.''

Keel returned his smile and called in the reinforcements. ''Travis!''

When seconds passed with no response to his summons, Keel turned and looked toward the sofa.

The big man took another swig of coffee and shook his head. ''I'm sorry, Mr. Keel. But I don't need any job that bad.''

Keel turned back to Rob, his smile a memory. Then he dropped his cigar and used his boot heel to grind it into the living-room rug.

Rob's gaze automatically followed that action—something Keel had apparently been counting on. The businessman's first punch was an uppercut, taking Rob by surprise and making him see stars.

Blood trickling from his mouth, Rob staggered back and shook his head to clear it. When Keel came at him again, he was ready. Blocking the other man's punch, he threw a solid right to his midsection.

Keel's face turned fish-belly white, and he sank to his knees with a groan.

Rob stood over him, hoping the other man would get to his feet, itching to continue the encounter. "It appears," he taunted, "that you've let other men do your fighting for too long."

Keel glared up at him, making no attempt to rise to the challenge. "Have it your way, Emory. I can use my own phone to call the sheriff."

Rob barely restrained himself from hauling the man to his feet and hitting him again. "Before you do that, you'd better look into the penalty for withholding evidence. Because that's just what you've been guilty of all these weeks."

Travis chose that moment to get up from the couch and move forward. Rob watched him warily, ready for anything. But Travis only picked up Keel's hat and reached down to take the fallen man's arm.

"Get away from me, you traitor!" Keel grabbed his hat and, slapping the other man's hand aside, rose to his feet under his own power. "You'll never work in this county again," he said as he slammed out the front door.

As the sound of Keel's car engine faded into the distance, Rob turned to the bearded man. "If you need a ride, my pickup's right outside. I'd be glad to lend it to you."

Travis looked as if he weren't quite sure how to respond to that kind of consideration. Finally he nodded his acceptance. "Thanks, I'd appreciate that."

"You can bring it back to the Double Diamond tomorrow. If you like what you see there, we can always use an extra ranch hand."

There was another moment of silence as Travis looked at Rob assessingly and weighed his offer. "You don't know anything about me."

"I saw how you acted today, and that tells me all I need to know."

"Then you've got yourself a hired hand. I'll have to make it the day after tomorrow, though. Tomorrow, I've got an appointment to do some home repairs for Miss Lissa Jackson."

Travis pulled on his Stetson with a grin that made his big face look as appealing as a teddy bear's. With a nod to Jenny and Tate, he made his way out.

Feeling as if all were right with his world, Rob shut the door behind the other man and turned to face Jenny with a smile. It quickly faded when he saw her look of alarm. Tate's face had gone deathly pale, and he was clutching at his chest.

"Call Doc Hooper," Jenny cried. "Tell him Daddy's having another attack!"

She watched Rob disappear into the kitchen and tried to pry the cap off the bottle of heart pills with fingers that were suddenly numb. The bottle fell to the floor, and she scrambled after the rolling pills until she succeeded in catching one. Brushing it off, she pushed it into her father's mouth.

"I'm all right," Tate gasped, struggling to get to his feet.

"Daddy, no!"

Jenny tried to catch him as he fell, but his weight carried her to the floor along with him. She shifted her bruised hip and sat up, turning to cradle his head in her arms.

Rob reentered the room and squatted down beside them. "Doc Hooper is on his way over. He called the helicopter to airlift Tate to the hospital in San Antonio."

Jenny rocked her father back and forth as he had rocked her only moments before. "Get my bag, Rob! I need my stethoscope. I need—"

Tate put a restraining hand on her arm, stopping both the rocking and the desperate stream of words. "It's no... use, Jenny. Don't... try to fight it."

"No!" Tears spilled down her cheeks and dropped onto his upturned face. "No, I won't let you go!"

"You ain't... got no choice." His blue-tinged lips quirked upward in a smile. His words were barely audible, interspersed with gasps as he fought for air. "I... brought you into... the world. Did you know that, Jenny?"

Jenny shook her head. "Don't talk, Daddy. Please save your breath! The helicopter will be here soon."

Tate continued as if he hadn't heard her, grimacing and pausing frequently between words, but clearly determined to have his say. "That bastard, Parker, had beat Mary up again. Left her bleeding on the floor. The phone had been turned off awhile back, so

I was riding by to check on her. I got there just in time to help you into the world."

He touched her face tenderly, then his eyes changed, glowing with an enmity that the passage of more than twenty years had failed to dim. "I tracked Parker out to where he was working, riding fence on the Keel place. I told him that I loved Mary and that I was going to marry her. I told him that if he touched her again, I'd kill him."

Tate paused, biting his lip and groaning as another pain seized him. Jenny looked at Rob, pleading for help he couldn't give.

After a moment, despite Jenny's pleas to the contrary, Tate began to speak again. "Parker laughed at me, Jenny. He laughed and he said that if he couldn't have Mary, no man would. He said he'd watch and wait for me to let my guard down. Then he'd shoot me in the back and make sure that whore, Mary, suffered long and hard for betraying him before he finally let her die."

Tate looked up at Jenny, one hand clutching her arm. "That's when I lost my head. I drew my rifle and shot him out of the saddle. I wasn't sorry then, and I'm not sorry now. I was willing to pay any price for freeing your mother from that scum. But if I had gone to jail, there would have been no one to take care of her—or you. So I buried Parker and told everyone I'd scared him into leaving. Your mother guessed the truth, but after what he'd done to her, she only felt relieved that he couldn't hurt her anymore."

Another spasm took him and he jerked in her arms. Jenny sobbed aloud, feeling the pain in her own chest. "I should have gone through with the wedding," she told him. "I should have married Keel!"

Tate shook his head slowly. "I was dying, anyway, Jenny. You know that. At least now I can die happy, knowing that you have a good man to take care of you. Knowing that you don't hate me for what I did."

Jenny held him tighter, as if by doing so she could wrest him from death's grasp. "I love you, Daddy. I've always loved you."

Tate smiled up at her and gave a long, tired sigh. Then he closed his eyes, and his head fell to one side.

Jenny moaned deep in her throat and began to rock to and fro as the faint, unmistakable sound of helicopter blades rose up in the distance.

Rob watched her for as long as he could stand it and then gently touched her arm. "Jenny, sweetheart, you've got to let him go."

She looked up at him, the expression in her eyes as black and empty as night. "Go away," she said in a low, expressionless voice. "Go away and just leave me alone."

Rob felt a cold hand clutch at his own heart. Had he won her only to lose her now? Had he rescued her from Keel only to have her reject him because she blamed him for her father's death?

"You don't mean that," he appealed.

Jenny didn't even look up.

Finally, Rob realized that it didn't matter a bit if he stayed by her side or left. She had shut him out as completely as if it were he who had ceased to exist.

In the end, he did the only thing he could. Hurting as he'd never hurt before, he opened the door of the ranch house and began the long walk home.

Chapter Ten

" "Yea, though I walk through the valley of the shadow of death, I will fear no evil: for thou *art* with me; thy rod and thy staff they comfort me.

" 'Thou preparest a table before me in the presence of mine enemies: thou anointest my head with oil; my cup runneth over.

" 'Surely goodness and mercy shall follow me all the days of my life: and I will dwell in the house of the Lord for ever.' ' "

The wind carried the words of the funeral service from the white-fenced family burial plot to where Rob waited in the truck-lined driveway of the Landon Ranch. It had been two days since Tate's death, two days since Rob had spoken to Jenny. For two nights he'd lain awake haunted by the terrible darkness he'd seen in her eyes as she'd held Tate's lifeless body in her arms.

She'd told him to go away, to leave her alone. He'd promised to help her, to stand by her always, and she hadn't even wanted him in the same room with her. He'd fought Keel and Jenny herself to claim her as his own. But he didn't know how to fight this.

The service concluded, and mourners began to straggle past him on their way to the ranch house. Most nodded politely, keeping their eyes averted, apparently afraid he might try to engage them in conversation if they met his gaze. He understood their hesitancy. His place here had yet to be defined. Was he Jenny's loving husband and Tate's grieving son-in-law? Or was he the man Jenny had cast aside because he'd brought about her father's death?

Rob didn't know the answer, either. So he was just as eager to avoid conversation as the other guests were to avoid him. It was the only mutually satisfying relationship he'd been part of for some time.

"How's it going, old son?"

Rob's gaze focused on Will, and Travis, and the other hands from the Diamond. He nodded in acknowledgment. "I'm bearing up."

Will tugged at the knot in his tie. "That's more'n I can say. I hate wearing one of these damned things!" He cleared his throat nervously, fidgeting and looking generally uncomfortable. The other men went through the same repertoire of behavior.

Taking comfort from their familiar presence, Rob squinted into the distance and waited patiently for Will to get to the point.

"Later on—after the doings here—me and the boys were gonna stop in at the Busted Flush and down a few in memory of old Tate. We wanted you to know... well, you're welcome to join us if you like."

Rob understood their offer of support and companionship and was warmed by it. He looked toward the grave site where Jenny and a small group of mourners still stood, gathered around Reverend Thatcher. "I'm not sure what I'll be doing later, Will. But if I'm free, I'll drop by for a round—seeing as how you're buying."

Will grinned. "I was counting on you doing the buying, boss. It's a while till payday."

Rob shook his head. "Try Travis. I hear he saves his money."

Will scratched his head and angled a gaze up at the tall man standing beside him. "Well, that's true enough. But there's a reason for that. Travis don't go out drinking with us too often."

"That's right," Jesse chimed in. "Ol' Travis spends most of his free time workin' over at Lissa Jackson's house. Though you'd think he'd've fixed everything that needed fixin' long afore now."

Travis examined the nails on one big hand and tried hard to restrain a self-satisfied smirk. "I *have* fixed everything. Now I'm working on maintaining it. That's the secret to keeping a woman satisfied, boys. Good maintenance."

There was an outbreak of appreciative chuckles that trailed off into coughs and loud throat clearings as Lissa herself arrived on the scene.

She threw the suddenly red-faced Travis a warning look. "Good maintenance, huh? You'd better get a handle on that bragging, mister. I just might be tempted to break a part even you won't be able to fix."

"Yes, ma'am," Travis said agreeably, his manner clearly indicating sincere respect and more than a little affection.

Lissa nodded, satisfied with his response. She watched as the ranch hands disappeared into the house. Then she leaned forward to give Rob a quick kiss on the cheek.

"Don't let it get you down, sweetie," she told him, rubbing pink-nailed fingers along his jaw to wipe away the lipstick.

Rob looked into a pair of beautiful, red-rimmed eyes that told him more clearly than any words that Lissa mourned for Tate, too. "I'll try not to."

Travis appeared in the doorway, a plate in his hand and a worried frown on his face as he looked from one to the other. "Lissa, you coming?"

Lissa winked at Rob. "This is the man who said he wanted it free and easy," she whispered. "No ties, no commitments. Now if I get more than three feet away, he starts reeling in the line."

"Lissa!"

She rolled her eyes and started toward the house, still throwing words at Rob over her shoulder. "Any time you need a friend to talk to, you just call me. Y'hear?"

"Roberto?"

Rob turned and hugged his mother with one arm while Margret moved to his other side to share the embrace. They all stood there for a long moment without speaking, and Rob came closer to tears than he had at any time since Tate's death.

Finally, Margret looked up, her own eyes moist. "Todd asked to come, but I thought it best that he stay home. He kept saying that he wanted to buy you a hot-fudge sundae to make you feel better."

Rob grinned at the mock rebuke in her tone. "You tell him I appreciate the thought."

His mother touched his face, her own countenance creased with worry. "You will be home to tell him yourself, won't you?"

Swallowing hard, Rob looked down into the eyes that had always been able to see what was in his heart. "I don't know, Mama. If things don't work out with Jenny, I might need to get away. At least for a little while." He forced a smile, trying to make light of it. "Maybe you and I can see the world together."

Nilda looked at him intently. "You won't forget to say goodbye?"

"No, Mama, I won't forget."

His suitcase was already packed and stashed on the passenger side of his pickup. He might say goodbye from a pay phone, but he'd say goodbye.

Jude moved up to stand beside him and, with lingering, concerned glances, the women left the two of them and went inside the house.

His older brother's gaze probed his assessingly. "I'm gonna miss Tate Landon. He was a helluva man. You know, he was as happy as a soul-saving preacher in a roomful of sinners when you stole Jenny away from Keel. Told me so himself. You're not thinking you're to blame for his dying, are you?"

"No, I'm not. But then, it's not what I think that's the problem."

Squinting into the setting sun, Jude glanced toward the grave site. Then his gaze swung back to Rob's. "That's only one part of your life. You have a family and a job to do at the Diamond. You're part-owner now, and I was counting on your help in running things."

Rob gave his brother a knowing look. "You could run that ranch in your sleep, *hermano*. You don't need my help that bad."

"The hell you say! Who's gonna deal with those damned city people who don't know which end of a horse to feed and which end to clean up after?"

Rob held back a smile at the real note of distress in Jude's voice. "Maggie will be there to help. And Travis is a good man. When he's not around Lissa, he has the patience of a saint. Anyway, I won't be gone forever. I may not be leaving at all."

"Maybe not," Jude said, the look in his eyes belying his words. "But if it does come to that, you remember that the Diamond is your home and it always will be."

They were shaking hands in a sadly inadequate gesture of farewell when Rob looked over his brother's shoulder to see Jenny walking by with the minister.

Her eyes were red and swollen, but the rest of her face had a ghostly pallor against the black backdrop of her veil. Her hand trembled slightly as she clutched the minister's arm.

Rob wanted to pick her up and carry her away. Away from the waiting guests, away from this scene of death and sorrow. To a place where she could rest and learn to smile again. "Jenny..."

She looked up at him, an anguished, pleading expression in her eyes. "Not now," she said, her voice ragged with repressed emotion. "Please, Rob, not now."

The feeling of rejection was a physical thing. It moved through his body like an infusion of ice water, coming to a final resting place in the vicinity of his heart. He watched his wife walk away from him as if

he were a stranger, and hardly felt the big hand that
squeezed his shoulder in a gesture of support.

"Don't push it," Jude advised. "That woman's
strung so tight right now, she's liable to break apart if
you put any more pressure on her. I know it's hard,
but just hold off awhile. Wait till everyone else
leaves."

Rob knew that his brother was right. But that didn't
make his advice any easier to accept. He had already
waited for two days, and he was strung pretty tight
himself.

He took a deep breath and released it, willing himself to relax. "I guess I can handle a few more hours."

Giving his brother a nod of thanks, he watched as
Jude turned away. After a moment, he was alone in
the yard. Being alone should have seemed a little
strange to a man who had always felt most alive
around other people. Instead it felt familiar. It oc-
curred to Rob that, sometime during the past few
weeks, he had managed to grow used to it. And
maybe, all things considered, that was just as well.

Rob opened his eyes to a dark, moonless night. He
was sitting on the ground, his back against a picket
fence. A few yards in front of him, he could just make
out a darker, rectangular shadow. He'd memorized the
words on the stone slab long before he'd dozed off.
Tate Landon, Beloved Husband And Father. That in-
scription said it all.

He'd walked up to pay his last respects to Jenny's
father, and he'd stayed because he couldn't have been
in the same room with Jenny without trying to resolve what was between them. There, he would have
been a bundle of nerves. Here, something in him had

found peace and reassurance. So much so that he had been lulled to sleep. Now the sound that had awakened him drew his gaze toward the house.

A car was pulling out of the yard, leaving his pickup truck and Jenny's Jeep alone in the driveway. It was finally time.

Pushing to his feet, Rob said a silent prayer. Then he brushed off his jeans and started toward the house.

He pushed open the door and walked into the living room. She was sitting there alone in Tate's rocker, holding her father's old worn robe in her lap and staring straight ahead at nothing.

At the sound of his footsteps, she looked up at him with the startled eyes of a doe trapped in the headlights of an oncoming car.

Rob felt the same apprehension. Now that the time of reckoning was here, he found himself wanting to delay it, to postpone the inevitable. All at once, even the hellish limbo he'd been living in for the past two days seemed preferable to a final rejection.

One slim hand stroked the old robe in obvious agitation. Her voice sounded strained and shaky. "Rob, I'm sorry about before. I just couldn't deal with this then, with everyone else around. I—I don't even know if I can deal with it now."

Looking into the wide gray eyes he knew so well, Rob searched for some emotion that would give him cause to hope. All he saw there was exhaustion and pain. All he wanted to do was ease it.

"I understand," he told her, and meant it.

"Have you eaten?" she asked suddenly, laying aside the robe and getting to her feet. "There's plenty—"

Rob's indecision came to an abrupt end. He moved to intercept her, terminating the flow of her words in midsentence.

He'd left Jenny alone with her thoughts as she'd requested, given her time and space to decide what she wanted to do. Now he'd had enough of waiting.

"Jenny," he admonished softly, "we have to deal with this. Now. Together."

Jenny took a step backward, a step away from him, and sank onto the rocker again. The old wood creaked in protest. Closing her eyes, she let her head roll to the side.

Rob was filled with conflicting urges. He wanted to carry her to her room and take her as a woman, to make her his wife and bridge the distance between them in the most basic, most physical way. And he wanted to hold her and comfort her as he would a child, with hugs and whispered assurances. More than that, he wanted her to stop the cascade of pain within him, to tell him that there was still a chance for them, no matter how remote.

His heart made the choice for him. He sank down on one knee beside the rocker and looked up into Jenny's averted face. "Do you want me to stay, Jen? Do you want me to be your husband?"

Jenny lifted one hand. It fluttered up in a vaguely helpless gesture, then came to rest on the arm of the chair. "Rob, right now I don't have anything to give you. I don't know if I ever will again." She paused, searching her tired mind for words that would explain. "I don't want to think. I don't want to feel. But most of all I don't want to love anymore—not when death can tear that love away from me at a moment's notice. I—I just can't."

Rob's jaw clenched. He had come expecting her to say similar words. He already had his suitcase packed and ready to go. But now something inside him was urging him to fight to the limit of his strength before accepting her rejection. Despite all that had happened, he still believed in the future. He still believed in them.

He struggled to find the words that would give the two of them a chance together. "I know you blame me for your daddy's death," he said, facing the problem head-on. "Maybe I should have let things be. Maybe I shouldn't have forced the issue. But, damn it, I'd do it all again before I'd stand by and let you marry Keel!"

He had steeled himself for anger, for rejection, for anything but the near-hysterical laughter that came bubbling up from Jenny's throat.

She turned her head and looked at him through a haze of pain, pain so strong it eclipsed all other emotions. "Blame you? I never blamed you, Rob. You had no way of knowing what was really at stake. I did. I knew, and I chose my own happiness over my father's life."

Rob let her words soak in and felt an anger building up inside him that demanded an outlet. With an effort, he kept his voice low, his tone reasonable. "You're not being fair to yourself, Jenny. You—"

Unwilling to listen to his defense of her, she cut him off. "I know all the arguments that should take away my guilt. It was his time to die. The crime he committed was his to atone for, not mine. But I can't help feeling that I let him down. That when he needed me to protect him the way that he protected me all those years, I failed him."

"You didn't fail anyone, damn it!" Rob moved closer and took her by the shoulders, his face inches from hers. "You put yourself through hell trying to protect him the only way you knew. You nearly sold yourself body and soul to a man you loathed for him."

Jenny closed her eyes and shook her head in negation. "But I wasn't strong enough to see it through!"

"I thank God for that, and I know Tate did, too. You made the choice that your father would have made for you if you'd laid all the facts out in front of him. He was dying, anyway. At least this way he died happy, knowing we were together, knowing that you still loved him despite what he'd done."

Jenny wanted to believe what he was saying. Her mind understood, but her heart rejected his logic. It refused to stop hurting just because it ought to. She gave him the only encouragement she could. "I need more time, Rob. Time to try to get over this. Time to work out my feelings."

"How much time?" Rob asked, trying hard to be patient, trying hard to understand.

How could she answer that question when she didn't have an answer to give him? "I don't know, Rob," she whispered. "I just don't know."

Letting his hands drop from her shoulders, Rob sat back on his heels. His eyes narrowed, the anger and hurt inside him bubbling to the surface. "It's all an excuse, Jen. Just a damned excuse. You're still doing it, still holding back, still not trusting in my love for you, or in your own feelings. Well, you're wrong! I know my love for you is strong enough to survive this, and I'm betting your love for me is just as strong. Until I'm proven wrong, no matter what you do or say, I'm not going anywhere. If you need to think, you can damn well do it with me here.''

For the first time since she'd held her dying father in her arms, something began to penetrate the wall of numbness that had grown up to separate her from the rest of the world. For the first time, she felt something stir within her. Love? Hope? She wasn't sure.

She groped for the words to express it. ''I *want* to believe what you say is true. I *want* our love to survive. I'm just not sure that's possible.''

Rob held her with his gaze, with the very intensity of his belief. ''I have my suitcase in the car. If you rejected me, I was planning to go away and start over again somewhere else. But I won't—I *can't*—give up on us before we've given it all we have to give. All I ask is that you try.''

''You were leaving your family and the Diamond because of me?'' The ice that had surrounded her heart cracked and began to crumble. Feelings came rushing back like a deadened limb coming painfully to life. She was appalled at what she'd almost done. In her grief and preoccupation with her own pain, she had failed to consider his feelings. She hadn't realized how precious a gift she was trying to push away with both hands.

She hadn't cried since her father's death. The hurt had run too deep for tears. But now the release came. Tears filled her eyes and coursed down her cheeks like rain. ''Oh, Rob,'' she whispered, ''I'll try. If it means that much to you, I'll try.''

Tears in his own eyes, Rob picked her up and carried her, unresisting, to her darkened bedroom.

He placed her on the bed and lay down with her. Holding her trembling body against his own, he was surprised to find that he needed to be comforted as much as he needed to comfort her.

She reached for him, accepting the affirmation of life, accepting the love he was offering. Whether she deserved it or not didn't seem to matter anymore. She needed it.

He took what she offered, determined to heal her, determined to complete their union and convince her of what he already knew—that their love was meant to be.

They rolled across the bed, discarding clothes or pushing them aside. Hands, frantic with need, gentle with love, clutched and stroked and pleasured.

Rob took her mouth with his, forming a hot, wet bond that was a joining of bodies and souls. He felt her hands on him, moving down the smooth, warm skin of his back and over the tautly curved muscles of his bottom.

He drew in his breath at the sensation, then held it as her hands moved to the front of his body to stroke the hard, velvet length of his desire.

Bracing himself on his palms above her, he shivered with a pleasure so sharp it bordered on pain. Dipping his head, he captured the tip of one breast, teasing it with his tongue and lips, drawing it into his mouth. Suckling it as if he could draw the essence of her being into his own body in the process.

Jenny's hands closed around him convulsively as pulses of sensation shot to the center of her body. Moaning in response to her touch, he dropped to one side. He leaned on one elbow, his mouth continuing to worship her breasts as his hand moved downward.

His fingers probed the moist, aching core of her, first gently, then more forcefully, as his thumb circled and stroked the hard nub of flesh near above.

Jenny's hips seemed to move of their own accord, arching up to meet his touch as her breasts thrilled to the warm caresses of his mouth and tongue.

Rob felt a sweet surge of victory as she cried out and strained against him. He felt the pleasure flow through her as though he were a part of her.

Unable to hold back any longer, he moved up over her and made their bodies one.

Jenny cried out again as she felt his first thrust in every cell of her body. Nerves that had yet to recover from the stimulation they'd already received were bombarded with new waves of sensation.

Writhing beneath him, Jenny gasped helplessly as the waves crested and broke, filling her with ecstasy. And then he moved inside her, harder and faster, until they were fused together in a cycle of pleasure that had no beginning and no end. Until the world seemed to come apart and fall around her in glittering fragments.

With an incoherent cry, Rob shuddered and convulsed in her arms, and then lay still. Exhausted, he rolled to the side, taking her with him, unwilling to be parted from her even now.

He held her and kissed her, licking the sweat from her upper lip, taking her exhaled breath into his own lungs. Jenny was his, now and forever. Nothing and no one could take her from him again.

With this the last thought in his mind, he drifted into oblivion, holding his sleeping wife in his arms.

* * *

Rob woke up with a smile on his lips. His body felt sated and lazy, humming with contentment. His mind was filled with half-formed thoughts, every one of them optimistic.

Stretching leisurely, he yawned expansively. "Good morning, Mrs. Emory."

He reached out to embrace his new wife and found only empty space. His eyes opened to confirm what his senses had already told him. Jenny was gone.

As he sprang to a sitting position, a wave of panic surged through him and he had to restrain himself from shouting her name. She was probably down the hall taking a shower, or in the kitchen cooking breakfast for him. In a moment, he'd be laughing at his fears.

But that thought didn't stop his hands from shaking as he pulled on his boots and fastened the snap on his jeans.

Leaving his shirt where it had fallen the night before, he walked down the hall, conducting a systematic search of the house. By the time he reached the kitchen, he was running.

No smell of cooking food greeted him, no welcoming smile. He was alone in the house.

He slammed out the front door, descending the porch steps with a single leap.

In the barn, old Tillie whinnied a friendly greeting. The other buildings were so empty and silent he could hear the thunderous pounding of his own heart.

Outside once more, he squinted against the morning sun and scanned the surrounding land. Her Jeep was still here. Tillie was still here. Jenny couldn't have gone far.

Then he saw her in the first place he should have looked, sitting in the spot he had occupied for so long the night before. His heart slowed to a cautious, hopeful thumping as he walked toward the family cemetery and his wife.

When he saw the wildflowers on Tate's grave and the tracks of dried tears on Jenny's face, he wanted to rage against the unfairness of it all. The capriciousness of a fate that had taken Tate at the worst possible moment and left him to deal with the results.

He longed to reach out and touch her, but he contented himself with just looking. Her dark red hair glowed with banked fire in the sunlight, but her face was as pale as the white cotton gown she wore.

She returned his gaze, her gray eyes cloudy with emotions he couldn't fathom. "I've made my decision."

Rob squared his shoulders, subconsciously preparing himself to hear her words as he would the verdict of a jury who held his life in their hands.

Her voice was soft and clear in the warm near-summer air. "I was so tired last night. I was in so much pain that I wasn't capable of seeing past it. The only way I could ease that pain was to punish myself for what I saw as a betrayal of my father. Punish myself by turning my back on you and on the happiness we could have together."

He started to speak, to protest her conclusion. But she shook her head, signaling him to silence.

"This morning, I came up here to think, to try and understand what I'd been feeling. I realized that even if I punished myself that way, it wouldn't bring Daddy back. It would only destroy what he'd fought and worked for all his life—my happiness, my future."

She looked up at Rob, a new determination in her gaze. "Like my daddy—my true daddy, Tate—I did what I had to do. And I can't find it in my heart to be sorry." Giving him a tremulous smile, she held out her hand. "I've been Tate Landon's daughter all my life. Now it's time for me to be Robert Emory's wife."

Rob stood frozen in place for several seconds, not quite believing his own ears. Then, his heart singing with joy, he reached out and grasped her hand, pulling her up and into his arms.

He took her mouth with his, communicating without words his relief and happiness, and his hope for the future. Then he pulled back and looked into her eyes. "You'll never regret loving me, Jen. That's a solemn promise."

As one, they turned and walked away from the past, moving to face whatever the future held, together.

Epilogue

"Here he comes," Jenny said, announcing the birth of the foal that had been giving her so much trouble.

She moved back from the mare and let the slippery little body slide into the hay. Then she hunkered down to check the newcomer over.

"And it really is a 'he,'" she exclaimed, flashing a smile at Jude who was squatting down beside her.

"Thanks for your help, Doc." He looked up at Rob and winked. "Best thing you ever did for our business was marry a vet, little brother. Sure cut down on those bills."

Jenny gave him a mock glare. "Thankfully, Dr. Meyer left me other, *paying*, customers."

In reality, she was more than happy to render the service—and not only because she was family. Since she and Rob owned the Landon spread, Rob had never taken Jude up on his offer to deed him a share of the Double Diamond land. But the brothers had continued as business partners, splitting the profits from the horses and the dude ranch between them.

That dude ranch part of the business had even expanded to Jenny and Rob's place. In addition, they were also running the cattle on their land to give Jude more room for his ever-expanding horse breeding operation.

Jenny stroked the velvet nose of the latest end product of that operation, and felt a deep satisfaction with her work and with the people around her. Even the exhumation of Leroy Parker's body and the subsequent scandal hadn't been as bad as she'd imagined. She'd received nothing but supportive phone calls and letters, while Jack Keel had become a virtual outcast in the area.

She favored her patient with one last pat and gave a nod of approval to his breeder. "He's going to be a fine, handsome stallion, brother-in-law."

Resolute whinnied softly and lifted her head as if in protest. "And, of course, you deserve a compliment, too, Resolute," Jenny added with a laugh. "Same old story—females do all the work, males get all the credit. Right, Maggie?"

"Right!" Maggie looked down at her husband, the expression in her green eyes teasing. Then she cooed to the small, blanket-wrapped baby she held in her arms. "At least, that's the way it was when Karyn Diane was born."

Frowning, Jude straightened and crossed to her side. "I seem to remember someone saying she couldn't have done it without me."

Maggie looked at him in wide-eyed innocence. "And you thought I was talking about the *delivery?*"

Jenny looked up from the bucketful of water she was using to cleanse her hands and arms, and grinned at the other couple.

Rob gave an appreciative chuckle.

Only Todd, who hadn't once taken his eyes off the colt, seemed oblivious to the conversation. "Look," he exclaimed, barely able to contain his excitement. "He's trying to get up!"

Following his mother's example, the big colt hoisted himself up onto spindly legs that seemed way too fragile to support his weight. Tottering closer to Resolute, he angled his head and began to nurse. The mare gave a nearly human sigh, apparently thankful that the hardest part of her task was over.

"Can I name him, Daddy?" Todd begged, looking at Jude beseechingly.

A corner of Jude's mouth curved in amusement, but otherwise he managed to maintain a serious expression, as if he were weighing the decision very carefully. "I guess you're old enough to do that."

Todd beamed with pride. "Then I'm gonna name him Diamond 'cause he lives on the Double Diamond, and he has a white diamond on his forehead."

His mother looked to Jude, then nodded in approval. "I think that's a name even a stallion could be proud of."

The beep of a car horn drew them all outside. Lissa waved from the passenger seat of a late model Cadillac as Travis stopped the car in front of the barn.

Rob walked up to shake Travis's hand as the taller man uncoiled himself from behind the wheel. "So how is business in the big city?"

When Travis had married Lissa and moved to San Antonio to open a security and investigation agency several months before, the only one who had truly been surprised was Travis himself.

"Doin' good," the big man responded with a wide smile, obviously proud of his achievements but too modest to boast.

Then Lissa hauled herself out of the car, and Rob saw that Travis's smile had been inspired by more than business success and a new Cadillac.

Rob shook his head in wonder at the size of her abdomen. "I see ol' Trav is feeding you good," he teased.

Narrowing her eyes, Lissa all but hissed at him. "If I could walk, I'd come over there and knock that smile off your pretty face, you manure-kicking cow chaser!"

Rob couldn't help laughing. "That's okay, darlin'," he assured her. "I'll come to you."

He ducked Lissa's halfhearted slap and gathered her as close as he could for a hug.

Jenny stood by Lissa's side, beaming at the friend she hadn't seen in way too long. "When are you due?"

"It feels like any day now," Lissa told her. "But the doctor says I've got another month to go. If I don't burst before then!"

Travis came up behind his wife and drew her against him. "That's all right," he soothed. "You're the most beautiful sight these eyes have ever seen."

Lissa smiled and nuzzled. Jenny and Maggie sighed audibly. Jude and Rob both gave Travis a look of admiration heretofore reserved for legendary men capable of gentling truly ornery pieces of horseflesh and living to tell the tale.

Temporarily placated, Lissa waddled forward to peer at the gurgling, pink-wrapped bundle in Mag-

gie's arms. "This must be little Karyn," she said.
"What a pretty girl! I do believe she has her daddy's
eyes. But the rest of her face is the image of yours,
Maggie."

"Thank God," Jude said with sincere gratitude.

He earned a dark glare from Margret, but even she
couldn't resist joining him in the friendly laughter that
followed.

Looking forward to sharing the evening together,
they all turned and followed the smell of barbecue into
the ranch house.

"I shouldn't have had that last helping," Rob
groaned.

He shut off the engine and the headlights and
climbed out of his pickup, massaging an abdomen that
was as hard and flat as a Texas highway.

Jenny gave his dark silhouette an envious look before starting toward the door of their home. "No
matter how much you eat, you never gain an ounce."

"Neither do you," he protested.

"Humph."

"Well, we'll just see if I can feel any difference."

Eyes gleaming with mischief, he pounced, chasing
her and tugging at her blouse while she giggled and
shrieked, and tried to evade him.

Stumbling and laughing, he lunged up the porch
steps after her and managed to seize one slender wrist.
He used her own momentum to twist her around.
Then he leaned against her left side, pinning her body
and her left arm against the front door while he held
her right arm behind her.

Both arms restrained, her chest heaving, she looked up into her husband's face and burst into uncontrollable laughter.

He grinned down at her, enjoying her, and the night, and the sexual excitement that was beginning to simmer between them. "Something funny?" he asked.

"Only your face!"

"That joke is so bad it requires retaliation."

He slipped one tanned, callused hand under the hem of her blouse and let it slide over the satin skin of her midriff. "Maybe I should see if you're still ticklish? What do you think?"

Jenny's giggles stopped, and her eyes widened. "No, Rob! Please, don't!"

He ran one taunting finger down the center of her body until it met the waistband of her jeans. "What's it worth to you?"

A half smile curved Jenny's lips, and she gave him a come-hither stare. "Just what do you want, cowboy?"

Taking an unsteady breath, Rob popped the snap on her jeans and lowered the zipper with a speed that rivaled anything in the *Guinness Book of Records*.

His fingers eased beneath the elastic waistband of her panties and raised goose bumps in their wake as they trailed over her quivering abdomen. Circling, stroking, starting, stopping, beginning all over again, Rob took her to the edge and balanced there until his own breathing was as ragged as hers.

Unable to hold back a second longer, he released his prisoner. They stumbled into the house, wrapped in each other's arms. Pieces of clothing were discarded at random, mouths fused and parted as they made their way to the bedroom. They didn't quite reach their destination.

Rob took her down on the hall carpet, pulling her jeans, panties and shoes off in one violent rush. Then he pushed her knees apart and thrust into her until he could go no further.

Jenny felt a jolt of pure pleasure. Wrapping her body around his, she rolled him over. Then she pushed up until she sat astride him.

His eyes reflecting a passion that was growing too hot to handle, Rob bucked under her as she moved. His hands kneaded her hips and buttocks, then traveled up to her breasts.

"You'd better hurry up, lady," he warned. "Or I'm gonna get to the finish line first."

Taking his hand, she guided it downward to the place where their bodies joined.

She shuddered as he stroked her inside and out, feeling him everywhere at once until he seemed to envelop her with love.

Waves of ecstasy radiated outward from the center of her body, shaking her, shattering her control, until her very sense of self blurred and mingled with his. She felt his every breath, every beat of his heart, every pulse of his own pleasure as he gave her the essence of his being.

Light-headed, panting, spent, she fell forward onto his sweat-damp chest and gave him a lingering kiss.

Sometime later, they finally managed to make it to the bedroom. Snuggling spoon-style, they pulled up the covers and gave separate sighs of contentment. Rob reached up and turned off the lamp.

Then Jenny suddenly stiffened. "Oh, Lord," she murmured. "I forgot to tell you. I was at the post office today, and I picked up a postcard from your mom."

"So where is it?"

"Somewhere in the hallway."

There were a few seconds of silence as each waited for the other to volunteer to retrieve the card. Then they both broke into quiet chuckles.

"I'll read it tomorrow," Rob declared with a yawn. "What did she have to say, anyway?"

"She's still staying at her uncle's house in Mexico, but she'll be home to see her new grandbaby in a week or so."

"Seems like everyone's having a baby," Rob said softly. Then he realized that there had been something very like longing in his voice. Not wanting Jenny to feel pressured, he tried to compensate for it. "Can't turn around without tripping over a rug rat or a toy."

"So I guess you wouldn't want one of your own, then, huh?"

There was a suppressed note of gloating in her tone that gave it all away.

Rob sat up and switched on the lamp so he could see the expression on her face. "When did you find out?"

Jenny blinked up at him. "I took the test at Doc Hooper's office today."

"And you didn't tell me?"

"Resolute was foaling when I drove up."

"And afterward?"

"I was going to tell you as soon as we were alone together. But you, uh, distracted me." She gave him a tentative smile. "Are you happy?"

Rob gave her a gentle, reverent kiss that conveyed his feelings better than any words. Then he smoothed a stray strand of hair behind her ear and looked into her eyes. "Are *you* happy?"

"Very happy," she assured him. "It's just . . . well, I can't help but wish that Daddy could have been here to see his first grandchild."

Rob turned the lamp off again, settled down next to his wife in the bed, and held her close. "The best part of him *is* here, Jen. The love he gave to you. The love you'll pass on to our child."

He was silent for a moment, searching for a way to comfort her. "If it's a boy, I'd be proud to give him your daddy's name."

He could almost feel her smile.

"I'd like that." She turned her head and kissed him. "Thank you for being there when I needed you the most. And thank you for believing in us when I was hurting too much to believe in anything. I love you, Rob Emory."

"I love you, too."

Rob smiled into the darkness and thanked God he hadn't given up on Jenny. That he'd been stubborn enough and loved deeply enough to lay both his pride and his heart on the line. He'd bet everything he had against the odds, and he'd been lucky enough to win it all.

* * * * *

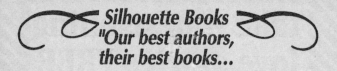

Silhouette Books
"Our best authors,
their best books...

DIANA PALMER
Soldier of Fortune in February

ELIZABETH LOWELL
Dark Fire in February

LINDA LAEL MILLER
Ragged Rainbow in March

JOAN HOHL
California Copper in March

LINDA HOWARD
An Independent Wife in April

HEATHER GRAHAM POZZESSERE
Double Entendre in April

When it comes to passion,
we wrote the book.

Take 4 bestselling love stories FREE

Plus get a FREE surprise gift!

HE'S MORE THAN A MAN,
HE'S ONE OF OUR

Fabulous Fathers

CALEB'S SON
by Laurie Paige

Handsome widower Caleb Remmick had a business to run and a son to raise—alone. Finding help wasn't easy—especially when the only one offering was Eden Sommers. Years ago he'd asked for her hand, but Eden refused to live with his workaholic ways. Now his son, Josh, needed someone, and Eden was the only woman he'd ever trust—and the only woman he'd ever loved....

Look for *Caleb's Son* by Laurie Paige, available in March.

Fall in love with our **Fabulous Fathers!**

Silhouette
ROMANCE™

SILHOUETTE... Where Passion Lives

Don't miss these Silhouette favorites by some of our most distinguished authors! And now you can receive a discount by ordering two or more titles!

SD	#05772	FOUND FATHER by Justine Davis	$2.89 ☐
SD	#05783	DEVIL OR ANGEL by Audra Adams	$2.89 ☐
SD	#05786	QUICKSAND by Jennifer Greene	$2.89 ☐
SD	#05796	CAMERON by Beverly Barton	$2.99 ☐
IM	#07481	FIREBRAND by Paula Detmer Riggs	$3.39 ☐
IM	#07502	CLOUD MAN by Barbara Faith	$3.50 ☐
IM	#07505	HELL ON WHEELS by Naomi Horton	$3.50 ☐
IM	#07512	SWEET ANNIE'S PASS by Marilyn Pappano	$3.50 ☐
SE	#09791	THE CAT THAT LIVED ON PARK AVENUE by Tracy Sinclair	$3.39 ☐
SE	#09793	FULL OF GRACE by Ginna Ferris	$3.39 ☐
SE	#09822	WHEN SOMEBODY WANTS by Trisha Alexander	$3.50 ☐
SE	#09841	ON HER OWN by Pat Warren	$3.50 ☐
SR	#08866	PALACE CITY PRINCE by Arlene James	$2.69 ☐
SR	#08916	UNCLE DADDY by Kasey Michaels	$2.69 ☐
SR	#08948	MORE THAN YOU KNOW by Phyllis Halldorson	$2.75 ☐
SR	#08954	HERO IN DISGUISE by Stella Bagwell	$2.75 ☐
SS	#27006	NIGHT MIST by Helen R. Myers	$3.50 ☐
SS	#27010	IMMINENT THUNDER by Rachel Lee	$3.50 ☐
SS	#27015	FOOTSTEPS IN THE NIGHT by Lee Karr	$3.50 ☐
SS	#27020	DREAM A DEADLY DREAM by Allie Harrison	$3.50 ☐

(limited quantities available on certain titles)

AMOUNT	$
DEDUCT: **10% DISCOUNT FOR 2+ BOOKS**	$_____
POSTAGE & HANDLING	$_____
($1.00 for one book, 50¢ for each additional)	
APPLICABLE TAXES*	$_____
TOTAL PAYABLE	$_____
(check or money order—please do not send cash)	

To order, complete this form and send it, along with a check or money order for the total above, payable to Silhouette Books, to: **In the U.S.:** 3010 Walden Avenue, P.O. Box 9077, Buffalo, NY 14269-9077; **In Canada:** P.O. Box 636, Fort Erie, Ontario, L2A 5X3.

Name: _____

Address: _____ City: _____

State/Prov.: _____ Zip/Postal Code: _____

*New York residents remit applicable sales taxes.
  Canadian residents remit applicable GST and provincial taxes.   SBACK-JM

Silhouette®

It's our 1000th
Silhouette Romance
and we're celebrating!

Join us for a special collection of love stories by the authors you've loved for years, and new favorites you've just discovered.

**It's a celebration just for you,
with wonderful books by
Diana Palmer, Suzanne Carey,
Tracy Sinclair, Marie Ferrarella,
Debbie Macomber, Laurie Paige,
Annette Broadrick, Elizabeth August
and MORE!**

Silhouette Romance...vibrant, fun and emotionally rich! Take another look at us!

As part of the celebration, readers can receive a FREE gift AND enter our exciting sweepstakes to win a grand prize of $1000! Look for more details in all March Silhouette series titles.

**You'll fall in love all over again
with Silhouette Romance!**

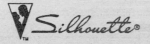

As seen on TV!
Free Gift Offer

With a Free Gift proof-of-purchase from any Silhouette® book, you can receive a beautiful cubic zirconia pendant.

This gorgeous marquise-shaped stone is a genuine cubic zirconia—accented by an 18" gold tone necklace.

(Approximate retail value $19.95)

Send for yours today...
compliments of ▼ *Silhouette*®
™

To receive your free gift, a cubic zirconia pendant, send us one original proof-of-purchase, photocopies not accepted, from the back of any Silhouette Romance™, Silhouette Desire®, Silhouette Special Edition®, Silhouette Intimate Moments® or Silhouette Shadows™ title for January, February or March 1994 at your favorite retail outlet, together with the Free Gift Certificate, plus a check or money order for $2.50 (do not send cash) to cover postage and handling, payable to Silhouette Free Gift Offer. We will send you the specified gift. Allow 6 to 8 weeks for delivery. Offer good until March 31st, 1994 or while quantities last. Offer valid in the U.S. and Canada only.

Free Gift Certificate

Name: _____

Address: _____

City: _____ State/Province: _____ Zip/Postal Code: _____

Mail this certificate, one proof-of-purchase and a check or money order for postage and handling to: SILHOUETTE FREE GIFT OFFER 1994. In the U.S.: 3010 Walden Avenue, P.O. Box 9057, Buffalo NY 14269-9057. In Canada: P.O. Box 622, Fort Erie, Ontario L2Z 5X3

FREE GIFT OFFER   079-KBZ

ONE PROOF-OF-PURCHASE
To collect your fabulous FREE GIFT, a cubic zirconia pendant, you must include this original proof-of-purchase for each gift with the properly completed Free Gift Certificate.

079-KBZ